Will's
d the
owing
game. Of course, Gina, Cherie, and Melissa
were with a group of his football teammates, and they
were all stationed in ideal viewing position to watch
him and Jessica. Gina's hand was on Melissa's shoulder
while Cherie had locked a full-on death glare in their
direction.

Will turned around again. "Jessica, don't—"

"I have to get to my locker before class anyway,"
Jessica said. "We'll get together Friday night, I
promise." She picked up her tray and stood.

"Jessica—," Will protested.

She bent over and gave him a kiss on the cheek.
"I'll see you."

Will watched her walk a couple of steps, then
glanced at Melissa's pale face in the distance. Great.
Jessica was giving him a crash course in Modern
Woman 101, right in front of Melissa's eyes.

And as of now, he was hovering somewhere
around a C-plus.

Don't miss any of the books in SWEET VALLEY HIGH
SENIOR YEAR, an exciting series from Bantam Books!

*Visit the Official Sweet Valley Web Site on the Internet at:*

**http://www.sweetvalley.com**

Francine Pascal's

# senioryear

# All About Love

## CREATED BY
## FRANCINE PASCAL

BANTAM BOOKS
NEW YORK · TORONTO · LONDON · SYDNEY · AUCKLAND

RL: 6, AGES 012 AND UP

ALL ABOUT LOVE
*A Bantam Book / January 2000*

*Sweet Valley High® is a registered trademark of Francine Pascal.*
*Conceived by Francine Pascal.*
*Cover photography by Michael Segal.*

Produced by 17th Street Productions, Inc.
33 West 17th Street
New York, NY 10011.

ISBN: 0-553-49312-4

**Visit us on the Web! www.randomhouse.com/teens**

*Published simultaneously in the United States and Canada*

Bantam Books is an imprint of Random House Children's Books, a
division of Random House, Inc. BANTAM BOOKS and the rooster
colophon are registered trademarks of Random House, Inc. Bantam Books,
1540 Broadway, New York, New York 10036.

PRINTED IN THE UNITED STATES OF AMERICA

OPM    0 9 8 7 6 5 4 3 2 1

*To Alice Elizabeth Wenk*

# Jessica Wakefield

I don't know how much longer I can handle watching Liz in teen-rebellion mode. At first, I was just psyched to see that she was mortal like the rest of us and that she gets fed up with parents and rules and all that. But now I'm worried. It doesn't seem like a phase anymore — she's becoming a totally different person. Kind of like if a cute little caterpillar broke out of its cocoon and it wasn't a butterfly, but a dragonfly.

All right, bad analogy, but you know what I mean.

# Conner McDermott

Liz is an idiot.
And I'm still in love with her.

# Elizabeth Wakefield

The tip jar at House of Java says Karma Is a Boomerang. If that's true, then my karma boomerang is coming back around full speed. Or maybe it's going away full speed. What I mean is: This last month has been a nightmare. After glimmering traces of hope, I lost Conner. And then everything else started to slip. My grades. My relationship with my parents. My healthy outlook on life. Everything.

But now my life's back in full swing. Or actually, most of it is still in shambles, but it doesn't matter. Because I have Conner. And that compensates for a month of hell.

Of course, I should probably keep my eye on that boomerang.

# CHAPTER
## Temporary Insanity

**1**

Conner McDermott turned off the lights and let his black Mustang roll to a stop at the top of the Wakefields' driveway. He turned to Elizabeth. She was biting her lower lip, her blue-green eyes alight with what could only be called wonder. Conner opened his mouth to speak, but he focused a moment too long on Elizabeth's lips, and the words vanished.

*Why does she have to be so damn beautiful?* Conner thought, turning his gaze from Elizabeth to his own hands. They looked ridiculous—still stuck to the steering wheel, as if glued there by the film of sweat on his palms. He quickly pulled them free and clapped, hoping to force himself into saying something.

"Well—" They both said it in unison.

Conner looked over at Elizabeth, and she laughed. "You go ahead," she said.

"It's been . . ." Conner hesitated, searching for the right adjective. He quickly wiped his hands on his jeans. "Interesting," he finished. That was definitely the word. Who would have thought he'd be smuggling Elizabeth out of a party that was being busted by the cops? Not to mention the fact that she was drunk, although the ride home seemed to have sobered her up. Talk about a role reversal.

"Yeah," Elizabeth replied, nodding. Her smile straightened a little. "I'm not sure if I can handle much more drama today."

"Well," Conner said, tapping his hands against his thighs. "I guess we should get you inside."

"I think I'd rather stay out here," Elizabeth said.

Conner's heart thumped against his chest. "What?"

"Oh," Elizabeth said, her face reddening, "I'm just not looking forward to sneaking around my house, knowing that my parents could wake up and ground me for another couple of months."

Conner looked down at the leather upholstery strip that separated his seat from Elizabeth's. All he had to do was cross that line—eight inches of leather—to kiss her. But did he even want to? They had already kissed once tonight. If they did it again, Elizabeth might read between the lines and expect him to start acting like the *b*-word. She'd want him to call every night—just to check in and say hi. Awful. Still, he'd better do something quick because the tightness in his stomach was starting to make him feel sick.

"Conner?" Elizabeth said softly.

"Yeah?"

Elizabeth slid over and put her hand over his, her fingertips lightly brushing his thigh. "Thanks," she said quietly. Conner felt the warmth from

2

Elizabeth's hand crawling up his spine, making him rigid with expectation. Was *she* going to kiss *him?* "Thank you for getting me out of there. Thanks for everything."

"No problem," Conner replied, trying to keep his cool. He stared at her delicate cheekbone, the little heart pendant that had fallen into the hollow at the base of her neck, the tiny dot of moisture on her upper lip. Just as he was about to lean forward, Elizabeth lost patience and sank back into her seat.

Conner took a deep breath. "Come on," he said. "Let's get this over with."

Conner gently lifted up his door handle and stepped out. He strolled slowly toward the big shadow of the house, occasionally stealing a glimpse of Elizabeth in the moonlight. Soft, blond hair wisping around her lightly tanned face, intense blue-green eyes, perfect lips. He realized he hadn't *really* looked at her in a long time—which explained how he had kept his distance up until now.

Conner grabbed Elizabeth's hand and led her to the front stairs. She stopped on the bottom step and jangled around in her purse for the keys. In the quiet night it sounded like a five-car pileup.

"Shhh . . . ," he whispered. Elizabeth swiveled around and put a finger to her smiling lips.

Suddenly the door flew open. Elizabeth gasped, and Conner's heart practically stopped—he had the sudden mental image of himself flattened on the lawn by Mr. Wakefield in pin-striped pajamas.

"Liz!" a panicked voice whispered.

It was Jessica.

"What are you doing? Get in here before Mom and Dad wake up and disown you!" Jessica hissed. "Hi, Conner," she said, flashing a faint smile. "Thanks for finding her."

"Do you need help . . . getting her upstairs?" Conner asked.

"Are you kidding?" Jessica said. "Thanks, but she's already teetering on the edge of disaster. I'll take care of this. You get home while you still can."

Conner nodded. "Okay. . . ." He took a step back and stopped, feeling vaguely dissatisfied.

Elizabeth looked confused. "Good night."

"Yeah," Conner said. "Later."

Conner turned toward his car. He took a couple of steps and felt a hand on his shoulder. Before he could fully turn, Elizabeth was there. A pair of lips landed firmly on his, a hand washed through the hair on his neck, and a million little sparks shot down his spine. Whoosh. Then, as quickly as it came, it was over.

Elizabeth stared into Conner's stunned eyes. "Thanks again."

"Liz! Get up here!" Jessica half shouted.

Conner's feet were still stuck to the driveway. The foyer light clicked on, jolting him back into consciousness. He looked at Jessica and Elizabeth—both

4

were caught in the doorway, staring up at the top of the stairs. A pair of legs emerged on the stairway. The footsteps sounded like thunder. Mr. Wakefield.

*Here it comes*, Conner thought.

"What's going on here?" Mr. Wakefield demanded. Conner could see Mrs. Wakefield following him. *Damn. So close to freedom.*

"Tell your friend out there to go home," Mr. Wakefield said sternly, landing at the bottom of the stairs. "He won't want to be around for this."

Elizabeth turned to Conner, her face pale. "Bye," she mouthed.

Conner raised his hand in an almost wave. He caught a last glimpse of Mr. Wakefield's angry glare as he shut the door. Conner stared at the house for a moment, his heart racing.

*What is* wrong *with me?* he wondered. This wasn't his problem.

He forced himself to turn around, walk to the driveway, and wedge himself into his car. Through the thin curtains in the front windows he could see shadows moving. With the three-quarters moon above, it looked like a scene from a horror movie. Elizabeth was pretty much done. And so was he. His reputation with the Wakefields was toast.

But even worse than that realization was the one that Conner had a moment later—the realization that he actually cared.

\*       \*       \*

"Jessica, you're excused for the time being," Mr. Wakefield said flatly as Elizabeth's mother joined them in the foyer.

Jessica flashed Elizabeth a sympathetic look on her way up the stairs. Elizabeth pleaded silently in return, *Don't leave me here, Jess.*

"Elizabeth, you've got some explaining to do," Mr. Wakefield said in an eerily calm tone.

Elizabeth's mind raced through a thousand excuses. *I had to talk to Conner. . . . You can't keep me jailed in this house. . . . Temporary insanity?* They all seemed like wrong answers to a multiple-choice question, so she just stood silent, her eyes fixed on the floor.

"Elizabeth!" her dad prodded.

Elizabeth shot a pitiful look at her mother, hoping for support, or sympathy, or something. But Mrs. Wakefield just looked tired and disappointed. No help there.

"I was . . . over at a friend's," Elizabeth lied. She still felt the woozy aftermath from the alcohol and the whole surreal rescue mission. Was it obvious?

Mr. Wakefield folded his arms across his chest. "You mean a *party* at a friend's?"

Elizabeth looked up at him. She had never seen his normally handsome face look like this—all pinched and scrunchy. She could even see his forehead veins, and his eyes were almost piercing. *Mental note,* Elizabeth thought. *Dad does not like midnight wake-up calls.*

6

"Elizabeth, is that alcohol I smell on your breath? Have you been drinking?" Mr. Wakefield barked.

"You've been *drinking?*" Mrs. Wakefield said.

"No," Elizabeth replied meekly, still looking at the floor. *I'm dead.*

Mr. Wakefield threw his hands up in the air. "Then why do you smell like a distillery?"

"I don't know," Elizabeth muttered. She sounded like an idiot.

"Don't give me that," Mr. Wakefield said.

"Okay, okay," Elizabeth said, running her hands through her hair. "I just had one little drink—and it was hours ago."

"One little drink! On a night when you were grounded. What the hell is going on here, Liz?" Mr. Wakefield demanded.

Elizabeth took a step back. She understood why he was angry. But why did he make it sound like she had turned into some wild, motorcycle-riding, boozing lunatic?

"Dad, I . . . Look, I just really wanted to talk to Conner, and I—I knew he would be at this party—," Elizabeth stammered. She could tell this wasn't helping her cause.

"That's your excuse? You're grounded, Liz. That means you don't leave the house and no one can visit you. Your mother tells me that you already broke this rule once today," he said, gesturing at Mrs. Wakefield, who was shaking her head. Her disappointed face

7

seemed to make Mr. Wakefield angrier. "And you broke curfew! This is unbelievable, Liz. . . . I'm speechless!" He threw up his hands and started pacing the foyer.

Elizabeth could picture her parents having a bedroom powwow about her disturbing pattern of behavior. What had happened to their perfect, straight-A-student daughter? Had she fallen in with the "bad kids" at school? It seemed so absurd.

"I'm so sorry. I really am, Dad. I only hung out with Megan this afternoon because she was having family problems, and I . . . I guess I don't know how to explain tonight. I just—"

Mr. Wakefield stopped pacing and glared at Elizabeth. "I don't want to hear it, Liz. I can't tell the lies from the truth anymore. Do you want to be grounded for the entire year? Is that what you want? Because that's what you're headed for."

"Dad, come on," Elizabeth said.

"You think I'm kidding?" he yelled back.

Elizabeth was struck by a sudden rush of anger. They wouldn't even let her talk. That was why she'd gone to the party in the first place—because she was so angry when her mother had refused to hear her out. After that frustrating argument the only thing Elizabeth could think about was getting out of the house.

Elizabeth put her hands on her hips. "Dad, you act like—"

"Don't take that tone with your father," Mrs. Wakefield interrupted.

Something inside Elizabeth burst. "In seventeen years I screw up *once*. I go out and have *one* drink at a party, and you guys treat me like a delinquent! Hate to break it to you, Dad, but some kids drink every weekend," she said, almost surprised at herself.

"Let's all just calm down," Elizabeth's mother said.

But Elizabeth was past the point of no return. She could feel the moistness covering her eyes, turning Mrs. Wakefield into a blurry ghost. The ghost seemed to be speaking and moving toward her. She looked over at Mr. Wakefield—he looked like a ghost too. Elizabeth's breath came in short, quick strokes. She had to get out of here—now.

"Elizabeth, are you okay?"

The soft tone of her mother's voice pushed Elizabeth over the edge. They were so disappointed in her, but she was so angry at them. She couldn't even begin to try to sort out her feelings. Silent tears flooded Elizabeth's cheeks. She felt her mother's hand on her wrist and instinctively shook it away.

"No, Mom, I'm not," Elizabeth said. "I just need to be alone. Ground me forever if you want, but I can't take this anymore."

Elizabeth sprinted up the stairs and finally let herself sob out loud.

Damn that karma boomerang!

\*     \*     \*

9

Jessica picked up her phone and dialed Will's number. She needed to hear a calm voice after listening to the family meltdown downstairs.

"Hello."

"Will?" she whispered.

"What's wrong?" Will replied. "Why are you whispering?"

"There's some crazy drama here at the Wakefield household. Liz snuck out of the house and went to Cherie's party to meet Conner. I've been covering for her all night long, but Mom and Dad busted her at the front door—and they're really mad! Here, check it out," Jessica said. She walked to the door, cracked it open slightly, and put the phone up to it for a second. Perfect timing—she caught Mr. Wakefield in an all-out roar. Jessica brought the phone back up to her ear.

"Did you hear that?" she asked.

"Wow," Will said. "What's Elizabeth's deal anyway? I thought she was supposed to be the mellow twin."

Jessica managed a laugh. "Yeah, she is. I'm usually on the receiving end of these father-daughter talks."

"You sound pretty freaked out," Will said.

"I am," Jessica said. "What do you think I should do?"

There was a long pause. "What do you mean?"

"I mean, should I go down there? Should I defend her? Or will they just ground me by association?" Jessica was pacing her room, gesturing with her free hand. She wasn't used to all this yelling, and she needed a voice of reason.

"I wouldn't get involved," Will said finally. "Getting them mad at you isn't going to help anyone."

Jessica sighed. "You're probably right," she said, looking at her closed bedroom door. "I'm glad I called you instead of Tia. She'd probably be rallying me into fight mode right now."

"They'll chill out soon," Will said in a soothing tone. "Don't make a bigger deal out of it than it is."

Lowering herself onto her bed, Jessica allowed herself a slight smile. It was nice to have that soft, smooth voice on the other end of the line. It definitely eased the state of panic.

"Thanks, Will," Jessica said. "You should have an advice column in the *Oracle*."

"Yeah, I'm sure Liz and all her friends would really appreciate that," Will said with a laugh. "I'm glad you asked for my advice, though. I've never had *that* before."

"Well, you better get used to it," Jessica returned.

"Is that right?" Will asked.

Jessica thought about his lips pressed against the receiver and blushed. She realized the pause was drawing out into the awkward zone.

"I should probably go. I feel guilty chatting away up here while my sister gets bawled out. I'll see you tomorrow, okay?" she said.

"Yeah, maybe at lunch or something," he replied.

"That would be nice. Good night, Will," she said.

"Good night."

Jessica clicked off the phone and sighed. Will was way more than a cute face with incredibly functional lips. He listened to her, and he seemed to care. Even better, he gave pretty good advice . . . for a jock. Will was really *there* for her.

Jessica threw the portable phone against her pillow and smiled.

*Almost like a full-fledged boyfriend.*

# Conner McDermott

Gary was still up when I got home. The last person I wanted to see.

But for some reason, I wasn't mad anymore. He told me he wanted to make a pact, and I didn't even laugh at him.

So here's the deal. He stays out of my face; I stay out of his. He doesn't make Megan any more promises; I don't try to turn Megan against him. She's a smart girl. She'll figure it out sooner or later.

And Alicia is on the next plane out of here.

So it looks like there might be peace at the old homestead.

At least until Mom gets back.

# CHAPTER
## Out of the Blue
2

Elizabeth squinted and tapped the snooze button on her alarm clock. Could it already be—tomorrow? Her head ached like a migraine squared, still echoing the alarm. She flipped over—maybe she'd feel better after another ten minutes of sleep.

A montage of images from the night before shot through her head. Dancing like an idiot by herself at the party. Running from the cops. Ducking into Conner's car. Seeing her father's angry face at the top of the stairs. Running to her room in a flood of tears . . .

Couldn't she take the day off? It only seemed fair. To have to deal with the aftermath of last night was just too much. Too overwhelming. Beginning with her dad's disappointed face at the breakfast table. And Conner. Oh, God. What exactly had she said to him? And why had he suddenly been so chivalrous and romantic last night after a month of avoiding her? Maybe he was just consoling her because she seemed like such a helpless idiot. Maybe it was all a mirage.

She could stay home and take a sick day. Yeah, right. Her parents would laugh at the suggestion. She *could* just lock the door and not come out. But then she'd have to listen to these paranoid thoughts, playing over and over in her head like a skipping CD. Was there any relief?

*Aaaah!* Elizabeth jolted upright and slapped her alarm clock. Apparently there was no escaping this day, so she might as well get up and deal with it. A shower would help. She rolled out of bed and grabbed a towel off her open bedroom door.

At that moment her mother walked by.

"Good morning, Elizabeth," her mom said tonelessly.

"Morning." Elizabeth noticed her mother's set jaw and immediately retreated into her room. Maybe a good shower would wash away some of last night's awkward residue. Give her a fresh start. She tried the bathroom door. Locked.

"Jess!" she said.

"I'm getting out right now. Hold on a second," Jessica called back.

Elizabeth clutched at her towel impatiently. Was it too much to ask for an empty bathroom and a hot shower?

"Morning, wild child!" Jessica exclaimed, bursting out of the bathroom in a cloud of steam.

"Hey," Elizabeth muttered.

"Are you okay?" Jessica asked. She wrapped her

arms around Elizabeth's shoulders and gave her a quick squeeze. When she pulled away, a faint smile crept onto Elizabeth's face. At least she still had her sister.

"Thanks. I needed that," Elizabeth said. "Hey, Jess? Could you do me a big favor?"

"Sure. What's up?" Jessica responded, tightening the belt on her silk robe.

"Would you mind bagging breakfast with me? I don't think I can handle Mom and Dad this morning. Just, maybe, grab me a bagel and meet me in the car—is that okay?" Elizabeth asked.

Jessica smiled. "No problem. I think parental avoidance is key today. I'll meet you in the Jeep."

"All right. Thanks," she said.

"No problem. And don't be too bitter—there's always Conner to look forward to," Jessica replied with a wink.

Elizabeth paled. Her stomach clenched at the mere thought of facing Conner. "Yeah, right."

"*Please,*" Jessica said. "I saw the love-struck look on his face when you kissed him last night."

*Love struck?* Elizabeth thought hopefully. But then she shook her head to clear the delusion. "With Conner, that doesn't mean anything." In fact, it probably meant he was going to ignore her all day.

"Right," Jessica shot back, smirking.

"I really don't want to talk about it," Elizabeth said, brushing past her sister toward the shower.

She closed the bathroom door and locked it,

16

her hands shaking from a mix of nausea, nervousness, and general exhaustion. This was going to be a long, *long* day.

"Hey, Liz! Good time last night, huh? You were the hit of the dance floor!" a voice called out as Elizabeth and Jessica navigated the crowded hallway.

Elizabeth felt the blood rush to her face and turned to locate the voice. Some all-black-wearing alterna-guy was leaning against his locker, smiling at her. She was pretty sure she'd never seen him before. Elizabeth forced a smile and turned back to Jessica, her face still hot with embarrassment.

"Do you know that guy?" Jessica asked as they stopped in front of Elizabeth's locker.

"Apparently we're buddies from the dance floor," Elizabeth shot back.

Jessica laughed. "It's good to see you branching out."

"Jessica, please tell me things are going to get better today. If not, I'm going straight to the nurse's office to complain of violent cramping," Elizabeth said.

"Come on, Liz, it's not that bad. That kid seemed legitimately psyched to see you, whoever he was." Jessica smiled. "Plus you still haven't seen Conner yet—"

"Sshht," Elizabeth said, putting a finger to her lips. Why did Jessica keep bringing *him* up? She had no idea the way Conner McDermott's mind worked. Judging by his track record, he would avoid Elizabeth like the plague. Or ridicule her for having

17

been such a blithering idiot. Either way, Elizabeth had already decided it would be better not to see him. She would prefer to keep her golden memory of last night's Conner than see him today and have it all blown to bits.

"Speak of the devil," Jessica said, nudging Elizabeth in the side.

Elizabeth followed Jessica's eyes to the hallway ahead of them and felt her heart kick into overdrive. Conner was ambling casually toward them with his bag slung over his shoulder. He had on a charcoal gray T-shirt and black jeans, his hair was tousled, and his facial expression gave away *nothing*. How did he always manage to look so collected? Elizabeth glanced down and became suddenly conscious of her hands. What could she do with them that didn't look ridiculous? She had no books to clutch onto, no pockets. Elizabeth finally decided to link them in front of her, bracing herself for Conner's inevitable onslaught of sarcasm.

"See you later," Jessica said, hurrying off.

"Hey," Conner said, leaning against the lockers. His eyes followed Jessica's hasty retreat.

Elizabeth smoothed her flowered skirt. "Hey. What's up?" she said. *Go ahead. Give me your best shot.*

"Nothing," Conner said. "Are you . . . all right?" He looked at her for the first time.

Elizabeth probed his green eyes for traces of sincerity. She couldn't decide whether they looked

18

concerned or just plain gorgeous. "Yeah, I'm all right. I mean, I've been better. . . ."

"Your dad kind of lost it," Conner said. There was the slightest of creases above his brow.

"You've always had a gift for understatement." Elizabeth let out a little nervous laugh. She couldn't help it. His apparent concern was throwing her.

"What'd he say?" Conner asked. His arm grazed hers, sending a rash of goose bumps up through her shoulder.

"Oh, *they* said a lot." Elizabeth twirled her lock, popped open the door, and turned to Conner. She put on a mock-serious face and imitated her parents. "'What's happened to you, Liz?' 'We can't trust you anymore.' 'When did you start this drinking habit?'"

*You're babbling,* she thought. But she was powerless to stop it.

"'Do you want to be grounded for the whole year? Because that's what you're headed for, young lady.' Things like that." Elizabeth rolled her eyes.

"That sucks," Conner said.

"Yeah, it was pretty much a nightmare," Elizabeth said. "I'm not looking forward to going home tonight."

The bell for first period rang, prompting a symphony of slammed lockers and shuffling feet. But Conner was still leaning against the lockers, staring at her.

"So, did they decide your punishment yet?" Conner asked.

"Not yet," Elizabeth said, fumbling through her locker for her first-period books. "But I was grounded when they caught me, so I'm basically dead."

Conner smiled his patented sexy half smile. "You're such a renegade." It was half sarcasm, half admiration.

Elizabeth laughed. "Yeah, I guess—"

There was a touch on the small of her back and a faint, intoxicating whiff of aftershave. And then— out of the blue—Conner pressed his lips firmly against hers. For a split second everything came to a standstill. Her breath was caught in her lungs, and her heart paused, midbeat. Elizabeth was just about to overcome her confusion and kiss him back when Conner suddenly pulled away.

"Later," he said.

Elizabeth was paralyzed. She nodded at him, purely out of instinct.

"Later," she finally murmured, but Conner had already walked away.

Elizabeth's lips were still parted, numb from the lingering kiss. The second bell rang, but it barely registered in her blurred mind. Bells and classes and books seemed trivial for the moment. She wanted to appreciate her good fortune while it was still fresh.

Elizabeth closed her locker and leaned against it. A hundred vague questions blitzed through her head at once. *What just happened? What brought that on? What should I do now?* Each question spawned more confusion, and there wasn't an answer in sight.

Finally one question lodged itself a little deeper than the others and grew, and the smile on her face grew along with it. Could it be?

Had Conner finally fallen for her?

Will Simmons leaned against a wall next to the cafeteria entrance, his muscular arms crossed as he surveyed the oncoming hall traffic. He had waited for Jessica here enough times in the past couple of weeks that he'd figured out the pattern.

Like clockwork. There was the Giggling Freshman Girls Crew. They came first—always an ego booster. They traveled in a pack of ten or more, and they all quieted as they passed Will. One or two girls would dare to shoot him a doe-eyed, admiring look before they all broke back into giggles once they entered the cafeteria. After them came a senior history class with a couple of guys Will knew from the football team. Then came the Bandies, a dozen or so members of the school band, some of whom Will recognized from games. There was a short African American guy, barely five feet tall, a pencil-thin tuba player, and a female drummer who looked like she could bench-press more than Will. But they were always too consumed by Bandie affairs to notice the hulking presence of their varsity quarterback. There was only one last hurdle before Jessica would show—the PDA Couple. Two kids with multiple piercings and baggy pants and always all over each other.

Will squinted—there they were, stopped at the end of the hall. Today their passion must have gotten the best of them because they were pressed up against a janitor's closet, lips locked. Which meant Jessica must be nearby. Will walked over to the window and pretended to watch the goings-on in the courtyard—he didn't want to *look* like he was waiting for her. One, one thousand, two, one thousand, three, one thousand ...

He turned back toward the hallway, and a wide smile spread across his face. Jessica. She looked as stunning as ever, golden, shoulder-length hair bouncing, her baby-T-shirted body half covered by a blanket of sun that shot through the window. This was the moment he had looked forward to since they spoke last night on the phone, and it was well worth the wait. As he walked toward her, a surge of adrenaline overtook Will that made him want to just grab her and squeeze. He tried to resist.

Jessica caught Will's eye just as she was passing the PDA Couple and covered her mouth, trying to hold back the laughter.

"What's up, Simmons?" Jessica said with a grin.

"Just waiting on a lady," Will replied. "Have you seen a Jessica Wakefield around? I've heard she's the finest this town's got to offer." He gave Jessica a once-over and realized suddenly that he could no longer resist touching her. She was just too close. He wrapped both arms around her lower back and

22

surprised her with a quick, firm kiss on the lips.

"Whoa," Jessica said, pulling away but gazing up at him flirtatiously. "You don't want people calling us the PDA Couple, do you?" She laced her fingers through his. "Come on, let's eat."

"I was thinking maybe we could sit out there in the courtyard," Will said.

Jessica smiled at him. "Sure," she said, looking out into the courtyard. "As long as it's not too crowded."

Will smiled back. It was refreshing hanging out with someone as fun and lighthearted as Jessica. She was almost the perfect girl—smart, beautiful, and cool. He didn't have to always tiptoe around and coddle her; he could just joke and flirt and be himself.

Will offered up his arm to Jessica like an old-fashioned gentleman, and she laced her arm inside his. *I just wish it hadn't taken me so long to find her.*

Will set his tray on a table in the shade and looked around. The courtyard was painted the intense yellow of California sun, with splotches of shade beneath a few benches and trees. It was hot, maybe too hot if not for the breeze that whispered past. Will couldn't tell whether the goose bumps prickling his skin were caused by the wind or by the beautiful blonde who sat across from him.

"It's so nice out," Jessica said, biting into her sandwich. "I'm glad you suggested this."

"Only the best for my woman," Will said, laughing.

Jessica narrowed her eyes at his remark but smiled. "How's that veggie burger treating you? Coach has been telling a couple of our big linemen to start eating those things—to shed a little flab."

Jessica turned her head and held a finger forward while she finished chewing. "They're good," she mumbled. "Wanna try a bite?"

"No, I don't think so. I'm pretty much a hard-core carnivore. Veggie burgers and rice cakes and all that are strictly off-limits," Will replied.

Jessica shook her head in mock disbelief. "So I really am dating a meathead."

"Yeah, I guess you could say that," Will said. He looked Jessica in the eye, and they both dropped their heads in laughter. "Let's get together tonight, Jess. What are you doing after cheerleading practice?" he asked.

Jessica's smile straightened. "I can't, Will. I'm going shopping with Tia." She noticed the disappointment in Will's face. "I'm sorry, but we planned it a week ago."

Will looked down at his plate, hoping to shield the obvious frustration on his face. This was getting ridiculous. He only saw Jessica at school, in hallways and cafeterias and gym doorways. It felt like they were back in eighth grade. If they were going to get close, it would take more romantic, or at least more private, settings than just school. Like candlelit dinner tables and movie theaters . . .

24

"Come on, Jessica," Will urged. "You two can go shopping any day. Why don't you hang out with your boyfriend for a night? I'll take you out for a nice dinner, anywhere you want."

Jessica's smile had faded, and her jaw looked tight. "Please don't pressure me. Tia needs me right now. Her boyfriend's gone off to college, and she needs to keep busy. I'm just trying to be a good friend here."

Will put down his fork. A good friend? How about being a good girlfriend? Melissa would never bag him for . . . All right, it was unfair to compare her to Melissa. But Jessica didn't even seem like she wanted to make this work. She just wanted to kind of hang out, eat lunch under the trees, and be *buddies*.

"Why don't you just cut the shopping spree a little short?" Will asked.

Jessica looked at Will gravely. "I can't do that, Will. It's not about shopping, it's about getting together to talk, and that takes time. It's rude to just bail on a friend like that."

Will slumped his shoulders and leaned toward Jessica. "I just want to spend time alone with you, that's all. Not around all these people." Will gestured at the clumps of students that had filled surrounding benches since they had been eating.

Jessica leaned in, placing both hands lightly on top of his. "I know you do, Will. And I want to see you too. I just can't today," she said, her voice soft and sincere.

Suddenly Jessica pulled her hands away from

25

Will's and sat back. She was looking past him toward the cafeteria, her face reddened. He swiveled, following Jessica's gaze. Of course. Gina, Cherie, and Melissa were with a group of his football teammates, and they were all stationed in ideal viewing position to watch him and Jessica. Gina's hand was on Melissa's shoulder while Cherie had locked a full-on death glare in their direction.

Will turned around again. "Jessica, don't—"

But Jessica was already gathering her things to leave. "Don't let them get to you," Will finished.

"I have to go to my locker before class anyway," Jessica said. "We'll get together Friday night, I promise." She picked up her tray and stood.

"Jessica—," Will protested.

She bent over and gave him a kiss on the cheek. "I'll see you."

Will watched her walk a couple of steps, then glanced at Melissa's pale face in the distance. Great. Jessica was giving him a crash course in Modern Woman 101, right in front of Melissa's eyes.

And as of now, he was hovering somewhere around a C-plus.

# Megan Sandborn

Conner's losing it.

Last night, when I was up late studying, he came home from some party, and I have never seen the kid so happy. Telling jokes, making fun of me for studying, talking about how great this weekend was going to be. And this morning he still had a bad (good?) case of perma-smile.

And with all the family turmoil—Mom being away in rehab, my dad living with us—I just don't see how he suddenly became so . . . cheerful. I have no choice but to be suspicious.

I think it's time for a little investigation.

# CHAPTER
## *Modern Woman 101*
# 3

Conner trudged, head down, to his desk at the back of the room. He took his notebook and the book *How to Write Fiction* out of his bag. There was a reading assignment for today—some Hemingway short story—that he had read in study hall the day before. He remembered liking it but for some reason could no longer recall a thing about it.

"So, what did we think of 'Hills Like White Elephants'?" Mr. Quigley asked, hushing the chatter instantly. The sound of rustling papers filled the void. Hearing the title of the story jogged Conner's memory slightly—it was a story about a young couple drinking *cervezas* in a little restaurant in Spain, discussing something. Conner opened his book to the story.

A hand in the front of the class shot up. It was Maisie Greene, the tortured-soul, scarf-wearing po-etess who sat front and center in class.

"Yes, Ms. Greene?" Mr. Quigley said.

"I thought it was incredible. The economy of Hemingway's words, the way that the couple danced around the subject, the way he made you hate the guy character. It was really moving," she remarked passionately.

Conner glanced around the classroom, noting Elizabeth's absence. She was never late for class, or anything else, for that matter. Was she extending her stint as rebel without a clue?

Conner was struck by the sudden image of Elizabeth stumbling down Cherie's driveway, blinded by the cop's flashlight, carrying her shoes in her hands. So ridiculous. Conner let out a little laugh and felt a couple of heads turn his way. He better start paying attention before Mr. Quigley ruthlessly embarrassed him.

"Good, good. And what was the subject that the couple was dancing around?" Mr. Quigley asked, looking around the class for a new hand.

Conner heard footsteps in the hall. He fought against the strong urge to watch the door but couldn't keep his heart from racing. *Chill out. . . . It's just Liz.*

She glided in confidently, as if she were being followed by movie cameras or something. What was her deal? *She's probably still glowing from that kiss this morning,* he thought, smirking a little. To her credit, though, it seemed like every guy in the room was staring at her. "It's so nice of you to join us, Ms. Wakefield," Mr. Quigley snapped as he flashed her a look of deadpan annoyance. But Elizabeth just bit her lip and walked by.

Conner watched her settle into her seat and tuck a wisp of soft, blond hair behind her ear. *Peach.* That's what her hair smelled like last night when she nestled her head against his shoulder in the car. Maybe it was the poisonous peach fumes from her hair-care products that had turned him into such a cheeseball. *"I wanted to thank you for being there for Megan."* He had said that to her last night. And then he had kissed her. Now it seemed like a mistake. She probably had visions of them sitting next to each other at the soda shop—one big milk shake, two bendy straws. What was he getting himself into?

Elizabeth turned her head slightly toward Conner. He quickly changed his focus to his book and started rereading the assignment. The guy in the story was trying to convince the girl that he loved her, that everything would be okay. Eccch. Exactly the type of conversation he hoped to never have. Ever.

Conner noticed, out of the corner of his eye, that Elizabeth wasn't looking at him. He turned his head a little more to get a better look at her. Okay, she did have great lips. He could admit that. And the lips did make her a pretty good kisser. There was something about the way she got swept up in a kiss that was . . . well, it just made him want to kiss her more. But so what? She probably spent all of junior high practicing her technique on a lipstick-stained mirror. She probably—

"Conner!" Mr. Quigley barked.

Conner jolted his head toward the front of the class. "Yes," he replied, noticing the mocking smiles of a couple of classmates.

"I'll assume by your blank look that you didn't hear the question. Allow me to repeat myself: What did you think of Hemingway's use of dialogue in the story?" Mr. Quigley asked again.

Conner searched through a thick mist of stirred emotions into the realm of facts. Stories, Hemingway, dialogue, people talking back and forth. Nothing intelligent came to mind. He looked down at his book and noticed an entire page of back-and-forth, one-line dialogue.

"It's very simple. . . . It, I mean he, uses simple, short dialogue to express a lot more," Conner said.

"Simple. Yes, well, that's true, Conner, albeit a bit *simplistic*. Can someone expand on Conner's rather obvious observation?" Mr. Quigley quipped.

Conner tapped his pencil against the desktop. Simplistic. Obvious. Was there some sort of conspiracy against him? Mr. Quigley was definitely in on it, and Elizabeth probably was too. And that old wench who worked in the cafeteria—the one that always gave him a cheeseburger, whether he asked for it or not.

"Yes, Elizabeth," Mr. Quigley said. Conner's ears perked up, and his eyes followed.

"I don't think Conner's point was simplistic. He was just saying that each word of dialogue is packed with meaning, that to understand the story you have

31

to read between the lines. Like at the end of the story, when the female character says, 'I feel fine,' you can tell that she means the exact opposite," Elizabeth said.

"Okay. Good reading, Elizabeth," Mr. Quigley said. "So there are emotions and meanings that take place underneath what is actually being said. It's called the subtext. . . ."

Subtext. Right. That's what he had meant to say. Conner looked over at Elizabeth. She flashed him a quick smile, then looked back at Mr. Quigley. He thought about what she had just said. Not the analysis of the story, the "I don't think Conner's point was simplistic . . ." part. What she was *really* saying. The subtext behind Elizabeth's words was pretty obvious. He didn't have to read between the lines to see that she was sticking up for her man. And that her man was Conner McDermott.

And for the first time in his life, that didn't seem like such a bad thing.


Andy Marsden read the big, block letters on the door's window: Guidance Counselor.

*Guidance, my butt,* Andy thought. In his three and a half years of high school he had been to his counselor's office every semester, and it was always Andy who did the guiding. Guiding the counselor blindly through a series of made-up excuses, apologies, short-term goals, and long-term resolutions. The point was to make the counselor feel like he was doing his job, like he was making a difference in kids' lives. "You're right, Mr. Trugoy. But my friend Angel—you know Angel Desmond—well, he's an ace in history, and he just started tutoring me. I'll turn that C into an A in no time. You watch. . . . Blah. Blah. Blah."

Of course, Andy hadn't met his new counselor yet, and Mr. Trugoy had been known as kind of a pushover back at El Carro. Plus now that Angel was off at Stanford, he couldn't use him for the tutoring excuse.

Andy opened the door and walked slowly into the reception area. Directly ahead of him was a high, half-circular desk with a bored-looking secretary behind it. To each side were doors with little nameplates on them, four in all. Andy leaned over the counter and smiled at the secretary.

"Can I help you, young man?" she asked.

"Probably not. Do you have any diplomas lying around back there?" Andy asked, jokingly inspecting the area around her desk. He noticed a nameplate: Mrs. Helton.

"No, can't help you in that department," she said, chuckling. "If you give me your name, though, maybe I can help you with your counselor appointment. That's what you're here for, isn't it?"

"Sure is, Mrs. Helton. Marsden's the name. Andy Marsden. I'm probably just being notified of another scholarship offer," Andy said, blowing on his fingers with James Bond suavity.

"Let's see here, Mr. Marsden," she replied, turning toward her computer. She tapped on her keyboard a couple of times, apparently scrolling through a list of names. "Madden, Maltby, Marks, here we go—Marsden, Andrew. Looks like you've got an appointment with Mr. Nelson starting in . . ." She checked her watch. "About five minutes ago. Why don't you take a seat, Mr. Marsden, and I'll inform Mr. Nelson you're here," she said, motioning to a chair behind him.

Andy sat down. Mrs. Helton got Mr. Nelson on the intercom, then turned to her computer. "Have you ever met with Mr. Nelson before, Andy?" she asked.

"No, haven't had the pleasure yet," he said.

"And a pleasure it will be," she said, grinning.

What did that mean? His new friend Mrs. Helton seemed to be warning him. What potential problems could this Mr. Nelson nitpick about? His two PE absences last week? Well, those were easily explained. He . . . got serious athlete's foot from those disgusting showers. Serious. Would Mr. Nelson like to see for himself? Hmmm, what else was there? Ah, his abysmal grade on that calculus test? That could be due to his . . . attention deficit disorder. No, he hadn't exactly been diagnosed for it yet, but that's only—

"Andrew Marsden," a voice called out.

Andy looked up. A stout man with salt-and-pepper hair and a powder blue suit stood in front of the door to his far left.

"I am he," Andy said. He winked at Mrs. Helton as he walked by.

Inside the office Andy settled into its only chair—a short, uncomfortable wooden frame directly across from Mr. Nelson's desk. The office was small and meticulously neat, with a huge filing cabinet and a few inspirational posters as its only decorations.

Mr. Nelson introduced himself with a firm handshake and sat down—his head positioned at least two feet above Andy's—and began leafing through what was apparently the Marsden File.

Mr. Nelson removed his reading glasses and looked down at Andy. "So, Andrew, what are your post-high-school plans?" Mr. Nelson said, his facial expression stern enough to be almost angry.

Andy hesitated. Was that a trick question? "College, just like everybody else," he finally said, shrugging.

"College, yes." Mr. Nelson rested his hand on his chin. "Would you care to elaborate? Have you applied to any schools?"

"Not exactly," Andy said, a little unsure of himself. A lot of his friends hadn't applied to college yet—what was the big deal? "I mean, I've got some applications," Andy lied. He frantically scanned his mind for the colleges that *fit* him. "Like UCLA, and Stanford, and some state schools," he said.

"Well, that's a good start. Had you thought about what you might study at those schools?" Mr. Nelson asked wryly.

*Who is this guy?* Andy thought. "Probably English or—"

"Because I have to lay it on the line for you here, Mr. Marsden," Mr. Nelson interrupted, leaning forward. "You have average grades, similar test scores, and no extracurricular activities to speak of."

Andy looked into his hands. *That's not a very nice way of putting it.* "Yeah, well, I didn't want to put all my eggs in one basket."

"I'm not trying to discourage you here, Andrew," Mr. Nelson replied, "just trying to help you focus." He noticed Andy's worried face and paused to think. "What do you think your role is at SVH?"

Andy looked at Mr. Nelson blankly.

"What I mean is . . . What do you enjoy, in school and outside of school, that you can focus on in the application process? What skill, that is?" Mr. Nelson asked.

Andy could no longer think. One phrase stuck out in his head, and he was too tired to search any further. "Comic relief?" he offered.

Andy glanced up at Mr. Nelson's face. *Oooh, that didn't go over well.*

"Well, I suggest that you cut the comedy, Andrew. Because the colleges you mentioned are highly competitive, and they get applications from thousands of hungry students from all over the country, even the world," Mr. Nelson said. "So if you want to stand a chance at those schools—at any school—you better come up with a realistic plan...."

Andy tuned out. Mr. Nelson was still making plans for him. Andy tried to let Mr. Nelson's advice sink in, to feel motivated and come out of this meeting feeling inspired. But one question kept emerging from the back of his mind.

*Isn't it already too late?*

*Manganimous?*

Elizabeth was sure that wasn't a word. Why were wanna-be writers always trying to show off their vocabularies? She had only been sitting at her official *Oracle* editor in chief's desk for twenty minutes, and already she had found nine errors. Even so, it was nice to feel like her old, disciplined, *needed* self again.

Elizabeth scanned the room—a dozen or so people were gathered in small groups, discussing article and layout ideas. "Jen!" she said, locating the most diligent sophomore in the *Oracle* crew. "Could you hand me that dictionary over there, please?" Elizabeth asked.

"Thanks," she said as the dictionary appeared in front of her.

Elizabeth flipped through the dictionary. No *manganimous*. She flipped backward—*malevolence, majority, mainstream . . . magnanimous.* Definition: Generous in forgiving; eschewing resentment or revenge; unselfish. Hmmm. She looked back at the article, a personal profile on an SVH junior who started her own soup kitchen. Yeah, that word fit.

*Magnanimous.* Elizabeth thought about how strangely Conner had been acting. Saving her from the cops. Asking her this morning how things had gone last night with her parents. Kissing her three times in a twenty-four-hour period. Why was Conner being so magnanimous toward her all of a sudden?

Elizabeth shook her head. God, why couldn't she stop doing that? Every thing, every person, every *word,* all day long, reminded her of Conner. It was getting annoying. If someone could possibly tap into her thoughts and play them over the school intercom, the hallways would be filled with puke.

*All right, this is ridiculous.* She had promised herself to work hard today on the *Oracle* since she was sure that had been one of her parents' concerns during the blowout last night. But it was a little tough with her mind in constant Conner mode.

Elizabeth picked up the stack of papers on the corner of her desk. Layout. Check. Circulation. Check. Ad sales. Check. Sports editor. Check. Feature article. Elizabeth rummaged through the stack. Feature, feature . . .

"Hey, Liz, would you mind proofreading my piece?"

Elizabeth looked up. "Megan! Hi! Of course I will. I was just looking for the scintillating Sandborn feature." As Megan handed over her report, Elizabeth noticed the bags underneath her eyes. "How are you feeling?" she asked.

"A lot better, actually. I wanted to thank you again for talking to me yesterday." Megan paused. "I also wanted to apologize for Conner being so . . . Conner with you when he picked me up. He wasn't really mad at you. He's just protective of me, and he was probably a little jealous that I chose you to talk to about family problems—"

"That's sweet of you, Megan," Elizabeth interrupted, "but you don't have to apologize for Conner. I understand." *Great. Every time I think I'm out, I get sucked right back in.*

Megan forced a faint smile and looked into her hands distractedly.

"Are you sure you're okay?" Elizabeth asked.

"Yeah, yeah. I'm fine, really," Megan replied. She looked down again and bit her lip. "Can I ask you a question, Liz?"

"Shoot." Elizabeth furrowed her brow.

Megan hushed her voice and leaned forward slightly. "Well, I can never tell, you know, what the deal is between you and Conner, and I don't want to put you in a bad position." She paused. Elizabeth didn't like the sound of this—that karma boomerang could come flying through the room at any moment. "But did you go to some party with him last night?"

"Yeeaah," Elizabeth said suspiciously. *Sort of.*

"Did anything strange happen there? Because Conner's been acting *different*." Megan was almost whispering now.

"What do you mean by different?" Elizabeth asked, her jaw muscles tight.

"He was all, like, goofy last night," Megan said. "You know. All smiley." Megan imitated his ear-to-ear smile.

Elizabeth cracked a grin and covered it with her hand. Conner? Goofy?

"And enthusiastic—I don't remember ever using that word in association with Conner. I'm just worried, you know, because there's some history of manic depression in our family . . . and that kind of thing, the emotional roller coasters, the highs and lows, can lead to serious problems . . . drinking and who knows what else," Megan said.

Elizabeth tried to maintain a straight face, even though she was about to explode with happiness. Conner—chronic smiling, *enthusiastic* . . . It didn't seem possible. Was it because of her? Unlikely, but what else could it have been? Elizabeth tried to picture Conner with a goofy smile pasted across his gorgeous face. She couldn't. Momentarily the thought of living with the Sandborns again—in the room right next to a happy, smiling Conner—sounded appealing.

"Honestly, Megan, I don't think you have anything to worry about," Elizabeth said in her most reassuring tone. "Mood swings are just part of the whole senior thing. Trust me, I know. 'Seize the day' and all that."

"Yeah, you're probably right." Megan gazed at Elizabeth curiously. Her eyes were glimmering enough that Elizabeth began to wonder whether she *knew.* "So nothing out of the ordinary happened last night, then?" Megan asked with a coy smile.

Elizabeth was about to scream. Why was Megan torturing her like this?

"No, nothing at all," Elizabeth replied, one-upping Megan's coyness.

"Well, I guess that's good. I'll try to stop worrying, then. Thanks again for talking to me, Liz. You're the coolest," Megan said.

*No, really,* Elizabeth thought as she watched Megan walk back to her desk, *thank you.*

# melissa Fox

I have been patient.
understanding. Even nice.
But I'm not going to fall
over and die. There was
something in will's eyes today
at lunch—I know I saw it—
that told me not to give up.
Jessica had just walked off,
leaving him there alone in the
courtyard. He turned around
and looked at me dead-on,
those gray-blue eyes piercing
mine, speaking to me. They said
something like, "I'm still not
comfortable with this Jessica
girl. not like I was with you."
I'm not going to sabotage
their relationship or anything.
But since will basically begged

me for it, I think it would only be right to show him _why_ he was so comfortable with me.

Then he can make his own decision.

# CHAPTER 4
## No Sale

Elizabeth tapped a pen against her cheek, then scribbled away on the piece of paper in front of her.

5. Write an article for the <u>oracle</u> and be more vocal as editor in chief
6. Stop thinking about Conner during <u>oracle</u> meetings

All afternoon, ever since she had heard Megan's description of the new Conner, Elizabeth had been completely giddy. Giggly, goofy, can't-stop-smiling giddy. It felt like for the past month or so, she had been a balloon grounded by stress and worry, and Megan had stuck a pin in her and let it all out.

When she got home after school, though, Elizabeth felt herself being dragged down again. Walking through the front door was like revisiting an old battleground. Everything in the foyer had a mental image attached to it, and none of them was good. The cabinet by the stairs reminded Elizabeth of Mrs. Wakefield leaning up against it, shaking her reddened face in disappointment. The shining ceramic tile reminded Elizabeth of her father's pacing feet. The chandelier didn't seem pretty anymore but blinding and aggressive. And the stairs no longer seemed like stairs so much as an escape route.

So Elizabeth took the escape route to her room. She knew there was only one thing that would soften this anxious pit in her stomach. She needed a plan of attack.

## 7. Make time to talk with Mom and Dad

Each number she added made Elizabeth feel a little more competent, a little more in control. Where would she work? Not at House of Java anymore—been there, done that. Maybe at that cute little Italian restaurant—

Elizabeth heard a soft tap at the door. *Please don't be Dad. Not yet. Let me get a grip first.*

"Elizabeth, can I come in?" It was him.

Elizabeth searched for some viable reason why her father shouldn't come in, but none of the standby excuses fit. She wasn't naked, studying, or on the phone.

Elizabeth turned her list of plans over and straightened up her desk. "Come on in, Dad, it's open," she said.

Mr. Wakefield opened the door and shut it softly behind him. He hadn't changed out of his gray business suit yet, and for a flash Elizabeth thought maybe a lawyer had been called in to arbitrate in their dispute. She knew it was a ridiculous thought, but it still made her temples pound.

"Dad, I'm really not in the state of mind to argue with you right now," she said, surprised by her own boldness. The second it came out of her mouth, she regretted it. Mr. Wakefield looked pained, almost as if she had slapped him.

"I know," he said. He raised one hand, palm facing outward. "I don't want to argue either. I just came to talk, that's all. I thought about you a lot today at work, and I really don't want this to be combative. Okay?"

"Okay," Elizabeth said, softening a little.

Mr. Wakefield sat at the end of her bed and rested his hands on his thighs. "Well, you should probably start the negotiations this time since I did most of the talking last night."

Elizabeth exhaled. "Whew—where do I start?"

"I'll leave that up to you."

Elizabeth swiveled toward her father, wishing she had prepared for this as part of her little planning session. "Well, I guess this whole thing started back when I was staying with the Sandborns. Conner's mother is an alcoholic—"

Mr. Wakefield looked suddenly concerned. "Did you start drinking while you were staying

46

with the Sandborns? Is that where—"

Elizabeth sighed. "Dad, I thought you were going to let me talk here."

"Sorry, hon. Go ahead," he said.

"So, I guess I don't have to tell you Conner's family has a lot of problems," Elizabeth continued. "And living there . . . I kind of got . . . *distracted*."

Elizabeth looked at Mr. Wakefield. He had adopted his pensive face. Elizabeth suddenly realized that this was as open as she'd been with him in a while about her life.

"To make a long story short, I got too close to everything and everyone for Conner's comfort and he froze me out. It might sound stupid, and there were other factors involved, but losing Conner really destroyed me. And I guess I let it affect my schoolwork and stuff. I know that's not a good excuse, but it's true—"

Mr. Wakefield cut in. "So you're telling me you were involved with Conner while you were living in the next room?"

Elizabeth blanched. "I know it sounds stupid," she said, unable to look him in the eyes.

Mr. Wakefield laced his fingers together. "None of what you're saying sounds stupid, Liz. It's just a lot for an old man to swallow at one time."

Elizabeth smiled slightly. "You're not an old man, Dad. I know you understand, or I wouldn't be telling you this."

"Then why didn't you tell me before?" Mr. Wakefield asked.

"I tried. But you were too upset to listen," she said. There was a pang in Elizabeth's left palm, and she suddenly realized she was clenching her fists. She grabbed her pen and started doodling on a scrap of paper.

"So anyway, Mrs. Sandborn went away for rehab, and Megan's father came to stay with them, but he and Conner don't get along." Elizabeth paused and took a deep breath. "There's been a lot of fighting over there lately, and *that's* why Megan was here yesterday. She needed someone to talk to."

Elizabeth waited for Mr. Wakefield to respond. He was rubbing his chin like something important was brewing.

"Dad?" she urged.

Mr. Wakefield crossed his arms and turned to Elizabeth. "So what about last night, Liz? Is there something you haven't told me?"

Elizabeth's mind raced. This was an important question, like double jeopardy. She wasn't betting any money on her answer. "Last night I . . . I don't know. Conner freaked when he found Megan over here, and I just got really frustrated. I decided I had to talk to him and just got fixated on that thought. . . . So I went to the party."

"But that doesn't explain the drinking," Mr. Wakefield said sharply.

"No, I guess it doesn't. I was just frustrated and

angry . . . and someone handed me a drink—"

From the corner of her eye Elizabeth could see Mr. Wakefield's taut jaw muscles. For the first time in their conversation Elizabeth thought her father might lose his cool.

"This isn't like you, Liz," he said. "You don't let your emotions get the better of your rational thinking. And I've always been proud of that."

"I—I know—," Elizabeth stammered.

"I just want you to think before you do something like that, that's all," Mr. Wakefield said. "I know you're capable of taking care of yourself and of making the right decisions. So just think, okay?"

"Okay," she said softly.

Mr. Wakefield stood up. "You're not totally in the clear, you know. You still left the house while you were grounded, and you've been putting someone else's family ahead of ours on your priority list, which I don't appreciate."

Elizabeth nodded, stone-faced.

Mr. Wakefield stepped toward Elizabeth and stroked the hair at the back of her head. Elizabeth felt sentimental tears start to well up and immediately felt like an idiot. "I'll talk to your mother. Hopefully we can resolve this thing without any further tension," he said.

Elizabeth took a deep breath. Finally someone was listening to her. Finally.

*       *       *

Jessica rushed through the glass door and jogged toward the counter at House of Java. The clock behind the register read six after six.

"I'm really sorry I'm late," she said, huffing.

Corey looked at her huge plastic watch and sighed. "Ally was just talking about the cruel punishments she's going to institute for chronic lateness. Caning, whipping, firing squad, things like that."

"Very funny," Jessica said.

"Whatever," Corey shot back. "It's your funeral. Not that I'd bother attending."

Jessica jogged around the counter toward the back of the building. Ally was in her usual spot, looking frazzled as always. Straight, brown hair thrown up in a bun, a pair of old coffee-stained jeans, and a House of Java T-shirt. She was focusing intently on some number-filled sheet of paper.

"Hey, Jess," Ally greeted her. She looked up, smiled blankly, then returned to her work.

"Ally, I'm so sorry I'm late," Jessica said. That didn't sound sufficient, so she added a not entirely false excuse. "I got caught in traffic."

"It's all right," Ally responded, not bothering to look up. "I didn't even notice. It's slow out there, and Jeremy's covering for Amy, so it's no problem. Just don't make it a habit."

Jessica's eyes widened. "Jeremy *Aames?*" she asked, putting down her time card.

"That's the only Jeremy we've got," Ally said

flatly. "Amy wanted to go to some concert, so I called him because he's always asking for extra shifts. Why—is there a problem?"

"Oh, no, not at all," Jessica shot back.

*Except that he thinks I'm a heartless bitch.* She punched her card in the time clock and noticed her hand was shaking. Why? It's not like she had done anything to Jeremy—things just hadn't worked out as well as planned. She and Will were a better fit, and that was that.

Jessica walked back to the front counter, and there was Jeremy, grinding coffee beans. Jessica saw his profile and stopped in her tracks, trying to collect herself for the awkwardness to come. He was wearing an HOJ T-shirt that clung perfectly to his biceps as he focused on the task at hand. How did he always manage to be a lot cuter than she remembered?

The coffee grinder stopped, and Jessica felt like she was frozen in time. Her mind said to move toward the register, but her muscles got a slow start. By the time Jeremy had turned to face her, it was too late. Busted while blatantly gawking.

Jeremy flashed a semismile, then turned back around and started pouring coffee into filters. Totally awkward. Jessica's entire body felt hot, Sahara hot. She took a step toward the register, her mind still utterly blank. What did she usually do when she first came into work?

"Blondie, there you are!" Corey blurted out.

Jessica put her hand to her chest, startled.

"Cover my register," Corey ordered, pushing a chunk of dyed-black hair away from her eyes. "I gotta go smoke, or I'm gonna die."

"Sure," Jessica replied. She was so psyched to have a purpose and a place to stand, she didn't even bother reminding Corey that she couldn't order Jessica around.

Jessica stood behind the register, listening to the little rustling noises of Jeremy filling coffee filters to their premeasured levels. She could almost hear the bitterness in his brooding silence. Why was it that whenever she *needed* a customer, the joint was empty? She pressed No Sale on the register, and it opened with a clang. Yep, there it was. Just as she suspected. Money. She slammed it shut.

*Why are you acting like an eighth grader? Just turn around and say hi.* She had to admit it, though. There was something about this feeling—this stomach-in-knots giddiness—that was kind of fun, in a masochistic way.

Before she could talk herself out of it, Jessica turned around and started pouring herself a cup of coffee. Now she was right next to him. But his back was still turned at just the right angle that he was still out of sight. This was getting ridiculous.

"Hi, Jeremy," she said, a little too loudly.

He swiveled around and locked eyes with her for a drawn-out second. Big, brown eyes that seemed to

52

reflect all the light in the room. "Hey, Jess," he said, understating the moment. Then he went right back to rustling beans. How annoying.

"How've you been?" Jessica said, refusing to give up.

Jeremy turned back around, but this time he looked right past her as if she were invisible. *He must really hate me.*

"Jessica, someone's at the counter," he said nonchalantly.

"Oh."

Jessica hopped over to the counter and took the guy's order. Double cappuccino, extra foam. She walked over to the espresso machine and loaded up a double shot. Just as the milk steamer began to hiss, the phone rang.

"Jeremy, do you mind grabbing that?" she belted out over the steamer, in the kindest tone she could manage.

"No problem," he said.

Jessica finished making the double capp and walked it over to the register. She heard Jeremy go through the whole greeting rigmarole on the phone—"House of Java, Jeremy speaking, may I help you?" And then, after a cool silence, "Yeah, she's here, but she's kind of busy at the moment." Then, "All right, hold on a second."

"Jess, the phone's for you," Jeremy called out.

Another customer had walked in and was checking out the menu behind the counter.

"I'm kind of busy—could you find out who it is?" Jessica said.

Jeremy set down the phone and walked toward Jessica, his brown eyes burning. "I already know who it is," he said gravely. "I'll grab the cash register."

Jessica walked over to the phone, confused.

"Hello?"

"What's up, Java Girl?" a masculine voice on the other end said.

"Oh, hi, Will," she said quietly, turning her back to Jeremy. No wonder he was so irritated. "Is something wrong? Why are you calling me at work?"

"Don't sound so elated, Jess. I was just thinking about you, and I couldn't resist the temptation to call and hear your voice," Will said.

Jessica's heart fluttered. Could he be any sweeter? "Sorry. I'm not used to getting calls at work, that's all."

"Well, get used to it. Because if I get the urge to hear that sexy voice and I know where it is, I'm going to call," he said.

Jessica felt Jeremy's presence beside her, pouring a cup of coffee. The hissing sound seemed to convey his thoughts.

Jessica cupped a hand around the receiver. "That's . . . sweet," she said softly.

"The only problem with calling you," Will continued, "is that it makes me want to see you even worse. What time do you get off?"

"I think I'm supposed to close tonight, so probably

around eleven," Jessica said. She glanced over at Jeremy—he was fumbling with the espresso machine. A guy in back of the line looked at her impatiently.

"Oh, that's pretty late. Well, maybe I'll just stop by—I really want to see you, Jess," he said.

"I'm sorry, Will, but tonight wouldn't be a good night," Jessica said hurriedly. She turned around and noticed three new customers in line. "This place is totally packed. I should probably get off and help . . . my coworker here with the register."

"All right. Maybe you're right. I'll stop by some other time, when I can pick you up at the end of your shift," Will responded.

Jeremy glared at Jessica as he walked toward the register, arms filled with coffee and pastries. "Thanks for calling, though. I really have to go right now," Jessica said.

"I understand. We still on for tomorrow night?" Will added.

"Of course. I'll see you tomorrow, okay?"

"Bye, Jess."

"Bye."

Jessica put the phone back on its hook and hustled over to the register.

"I'm so sorry, Jeremy. I'll take over now," she said.

Jeremy's face was stolid. "Did you have a nice chat?" he asked.

Jessica felt her teeth start to grind. Jeremy was never sarcastic. Or did he really expect her to answer that?

"Ring up a latte, a raspberry steamer, and a coffee cake for this gentleman, would you?" Jeremy asked, brushing her shoulder as he walked by.

"Of course," Jessica said. She was overcome by the urge to grab Jeremy and say . . . something. Something to show that she hadn't totally forgotten about him. That she wasn't heartless. But nothing came to her.

And it didn't matter anyway. Because Jeremy was already gone.

# Elizabeth Wakefield

The turning-my-life-around list:

1. Get a job at some active, hip place where I can learn something new:
   A. Bookstore
   B. ~~The Riot~~
   C. Tabbouleh's Middle Eastern Restaurant
   D. Big Sister program (volunteer)
2. Have Mr. Quigley proofread college essay
3. Stop thinking about Conner in creative writing
4. Deal with homework right after school
5. Write an article for the <u>oracle</u> and be more vocal as editor in chief
6. Stop thinking about Conner during <u>oracle</u> meetings
7. Make time to talk with Mom and Dad
8. Find something else to think about besides Conner

# Andy Marsden

Since Mr. Nelson says I'm supposed to come up with The Plan, I should probably make some lists.

<u>Strengths:</u>
  1. I'm amusing.
  2. I'm a good friend.

<u>Weaknesses:</u>
  1. Everything else (apparently).

<u>Potential courses of study:</u>
  1. ~~Some sort of science~~ I hate science.
  2. Anything but science
     A. Literature
     B. Psychology
     C. Made-for-TV movies

<u>Potential careers:</u>
  1. Game-show host
  2. "Dear Andy" columnist
  3. Shepherd (Do they still exist?)
  4. Freelance bounty hunter (Did they ever exist?)
  5. Messenger of good tidings
  6. That guy who says, "Let's get ready to

rumblllleee!" before pro-wrestling
matches

7. Chief minister of fun

<u>The</u> <u>Plan:</u>

1. Make more lists tomorrow (and be
serious this time).

# CHAPTER 5
## Name Your Price

"Did you order the dung sandwich, McDermott?" Andy asked, bending over Conner's tray. "That stuff smells awful."

Elizabeth almost spit out her mouthful of salad. Why did Andy always save his best material for the moment right after a huge bite? She looked around. Everyone at the lunch table—Maria Slater, Ken Matthews, Tia Ramirez, and Jessica—were basically choking on their food.

"I believe they call it a sloppy joe, actually," Conner replied.

Andy scoffed. "Yeah, well, I can think of a few other names for it. You know, I really should go undercover and do an exposé on the inner workings of Sweet Valley High's cafeteria. Like that mystery meat with gravy that they serve on Thursday. If that's beef, then it's just a matter of time before we all come down with mad-cow disease."

"I think one of us already has," Tia said, looking at Andy.

"No, there's no medical explanation for the

phenomenon of Andy Marsden," Conner interjected. "Except maybe . . . genetic mutations."

Elizabeth wriggled in her seat at the sound of Conner's deep, throaty voice. There was something *different*, more captivating about him today. He still looked like the same old Conner—sarcastic grin, disheveled waves of brown hair brushing against the collar of his nonchalantly sexy old T-shirt. But his eyes were glowing even greener than usual, like a shallow ocean, and his facial expression seemed to conceal a secret that no one else could ever understand. Elizabeth felt the sudden desire to grab Conner and see those gorgeous eyes straight on. But she knew he wouldn't even look at her—Conner might never be able to deal with the whole couple-in-a-group-of-people thing.

"So, what's everybody got planned for the weekend?" Tia asked.

"I'm going to go check out that tractor pull at the coliseum," Andy answered. "Big Foot versus the Ferocious Four by Four! Monster trucks, trucks, trucks!" Andy said, imitating the echo of a radio ad.

Everyone just looked at him.

"No, seriously. Is there anything noteworthy going down?" Tia asked finally.

"I'm in geek mode as usual. I've got a ton of studying to do," Maria said.

"Me too," Ken said, smiling at Maria.

Andy shot Ken a doubtful glance. "Since when

have you been in geek mode? This doesn't sound like the Ken we all know and love," he told him, shaking his head.

"I've been picking it up a notch with schoolwork recently. It's weird," Ken bounced back.

"That *is* weird," Tia added. "How much of this time would you say was spent doing schoolwork . . . with Maria?"

Ken turned the color of a ripe watermelon.

Andy chimed in. "Yeah, it's almost as if—and I don't want to get too technical here—but the amount of hours you spend studying is directly proportional to the amount of hours you spend with Maria. Am I right?"

"All right, enough torture," Elizabeth said. "Leave the lovebirds alone." *All of them*, she added silently, glancing at Conner's profile.

"Well, *I* was going to visit Angel at Stanford, but he's going to some African American cultural conference this weekend," Tia said. "In other words, I have absolutely no plans."

"What about you, sunshine girl?" Andy asked Jessica.

"I'm going on a date with Will," Jessica said with a smile.

The table broke into the predictable chorus of "oohs."

"Well, how absolutely adorable," Andy continued. "And where is our fearless football leader planning to take you?"

"I don't know. . . . Probably to some restaurant for dinner," Jessica said. She looked over at Elizabeth. "Actually, I was thinking maybe you and Conner would want to go out with us."

Elizabeth felt a firm squeeze on her thigh and jolted against the back of her chair. She looked over at Conner—his reddening face buried in his lunch tray—and remembered that he had once called Will "shallow as a kiddie pool." He definitely would not be psyched for a double date with him. Plus no one else even knew she and Conner were . . . whatever they were. Elizabeth panned around the table. Everyone's attention was fixed on her as they waited for an answer. Couldn't Jessica have mentioned this earlier?

"I'd love to, Jess," Elizabeth said, scraping at the bottom of her salad bowl with her fork. "But I'm going to be grounded for at least a month, so we'll have to take a rain check on that." Elizabeth felt Conner's grip on her leg loosen a little.

But Jessica stuck with it. "Oh, I don't know, Liz. Dad seemed pretty cool about things last night. I'm sure I can sweet-talk him out of it for a night. If I can, you two are definitely coming with us."

What was she thinking? Had she somehow failed to notice the huge cloud of awkwardness hovering just above the table? Conner was digging into his mashed potatoes like he hadn't eaten for weeks.

"We'll see," Elizabeth said, desperately hoping for

a change of subject. Or a fire alarm. Or maybe a small earthquake.

Andy looked at Conner, a mischievous grin spreading. "Does this mean—strictly hypothetically—that if Elizabeth here were not grounded, you two would be interested in a double date?"

Conner looked up from his plate and gave Andy a look of death.

"Let me phrase the question more clearly," Andy said, waving his index finger at Conner like a professor explaining an important point. "Does this mean that you and Elizabeth are a couple?"

Conner leaned forward slightly. "Do you *really* want to continue this line of questioning?"

"Yeah. Maybe they don't want to be labeled," Jessica added.

"Thanks, Jess," Elizabeth said with an edge of sarcasm. There was a moment of complete silence as everyone glanced at everyone else.

"So, who's going to play with *me* this weekend?" Tia asked finally.

Conner squeezed Elizabeth's leg and then pulled his hand away. She looked over at his forced smile. What was going on in that head? Was he just so private that he wanted to keep their relationship between the two of them?

Or would this just give him another excuse to back away?

\*      \*      \*

"Liz, tell me we're not actually going on a double date with your sister and jock boy," Conner said. He had been holding it in since lunch, including the marathon walk from the cafeteria to her locker, but he couldn't handle it any longer.

"I thought that's what was bothering you," Elizabeth said, grimacing. "Why didn't you just come out and say it?"

*Why do girls always do that?* "I just did," Conner shot back, squinting at Elizabeth. "So talk to me— are we going to get forced into this thing or what?"

Elizabeth flashed Conner a pained look and began to fumble nervously with her padlock. "Of course not," she said softly. "You make it sound like a funeral or something."

"No, I know," Conner said. He hadn't meant to sound so snappy. "I didn't mean it like that. I would just rather go on a date . . . alone."

"You mean, by yourself?" Elizabeth asked, pulling her lock open.

"Very clever," Conner said, rolling his eyes. "No, it's just that—I don't want to spend an entire evening forcing conversation about eighty-yard touchdown runs and the swimsuit issue. It's not my idea of a good time, Liz."

"Oh, come on—Will's not *that* bad," Elizabeth explained, pulling a couple of books from her locker. "He's a football player, not a walking stereotype. Didn't you guys used to be friends?"

Conner tried to picture himself playing with Will when they were kids. It wasn't quite back in the sandbox years, more like T-ball and tag and ice cream bars. Anyway, it was far enough back to be in the girls-are-icky era of his life, which was too far back to still be relevant. Not to mention that sharing that kind of past with Will just made hanging out with him now seem more phony.

"Listen," Elizabeth said, interrupting his stream of memories. She turned and put her hand on his forearm. "We probably won't have to go anyway, so don't worry about it. I'm grounded, remember?"

It didn't sound very convincing. Conner could tell by the softness of her tone that she really wanted to go on the date. Or at least, she wanted to know that he would make the sacrifice just to be with her. That's how the female mind worked. And he hated to be such a pushover, but that soft tone, along with that delicate touch on his forearm, was enough to win him over. As pathetic as it sounded, he just wanted to say something that would make Elizabeth melt.

"How about this," Conner said, placing his free hand on top of hers. "If your parents let you roam free and you want to go on the date, I'll go . . . but you owe me big time."

Elizabeth's blue-green eyes sparkled, and she gripped Conner's forearm a little harder. "Name your price."

*　　*　　*

66

"*Hola, amiga!*"

Jessica heard someone shouting behind her, but she had just come out of a nightmare cheerleading practice of missed jumps, Coach Laufeld's impatient yelling, and a near twisted ankle. She wasn't in the mood to talk to anyone—let alone in a language she didn't even speak.

"*Hola,* Jessica!" a guy's voice called again. It was right behind her.

Jessica twirled around, instinctively ready to slap whatever rude, Spanish-speaking heckler was on her tail.

Will Simmons—still fully dressed for football practice—backed away, totally confused.

Jessica covered her mouth. "I'm sorry, Will. I thought you were—"

"Zorro?" Will asked.

"Exactly," Jessica said, laughing nervously to mask her tension. She gave Will a quick head-to-toe scan and instantly felt her nerves soften. He looked too cute in his football uniform—like a tough man and a little boy at the same time. Those muscle-hugging pants that looked too short, like he had outgrown them. The exposed bottom half of his six-pack abs. And last but certainly not least, his gorgeous, glistening face popping out of those huge shoulder pads. Yummy. If society would allow it, she might ask him to wear that uniform out on dates—without the helmet, of course.

"I didn't mean to scare you," Will said. "I just wanted my *chiquita* to know that I made reservations for two at Viva Zapata's tonight. You like Mexican, right?"

Jessica bit her lip and tried to look happy. She had completely forgotten to tell Will about her double-date plans. And this didn't seem like the right time. "Of course I like Mexican. I'm psyched," she replied lamely.

"All right," Will said. "I'll pick you up at eight, then. Our reservation's at eight-thirty."

Why did he always do that? He just matter-of-factly assumed that his plans were hers, as if she might not want to go earlier or later. Which she didn't, but that wasn't the point. She still wanted Conner and Elizabeth to come with them.

Jessica looked up at him and summoned up her courage. She had a feeling he wouldn't think this was such a great idea. "There's only one thing, Will. Liz and I were thinking it might be fun to make it a double date." Jessica noticed the changing pallor of Will's face and lost a little courage. "So maybe we could make reservations for four?" she eked out, scrunching her face and trying to look as cute as possible.

Will ran his hand over his sweaty face impatiently and sighed. "Are you kidding me, Jess?"

*I knew you would say that,* Jessica thought. "I'm serious. I mean, we don't *have* to. I just thought it'd be fun for a change."

68

"A change from what?" Will barked back. His face was red and indignant. "It's not like we've gone out enough that we have to start spicing things up like an old married couple. I told you yesterday that I want to spend some time alone with you, remember?"

Jessica looked at the floor. He had said that.

But Will wasn't done. "And why would I want to spend the evening with Conner McDermott, the tortured-soul rock star of Sweet Valley High?" he said, grabbing his heart with fake sentimentality. "I like Liz and all, but that guy's just too 'coffeehouse philosopher' for me. . . . Not that there's anything wrong with coffeehouses," he clarified.

Jessica looked into Will's pouting eyes and realized it was time to wave the white flag. Most girls would die to have a guy gush over wanting to spend more alone time together—she should probably be more appreciative. "I'm sorry, Will," Jessica said, tracing his forearm with her fingernail. "I could tell Liz that we'll do it some other time. She'll probably be grounded anyway, so it doesn't matter for now."

Will cocked his head. "For *now?* Are you saying that a double date with Liz and the rock star is inevitable?"

"I didn't say that," Jessica insisted. *But I was kind of hoping. . . .* "You can't deal with Conner for one night?"

"I can deal with him." Will wiped his brow and looked into her eyes. "But I was assuming that it'd be just me and you . . . and a little salsa."

Jessica just stood there and smiled. She preferred

hearing his deep, romantic voice to her own fumbling apologies.

"How about this," Will added, his voice softening another notch. "If, by some miracle, Elizabeth escapes being grounded, I'll change the reservations. I mean, we might as well get it over with."

*I should try the silent approach more often.* Jessica grabbed Will's strong, calloused hand and flashed him a sultry, lazy-eyed look.

"It's obviously important to you, and all I really care about is that we're together," Will said, almost on cue.

Jessica lifted Will's hand to her lips and gave it a little kiss. *One boyfriend down, two angry parents to go.*

Elizabeth paused at the front door to catch her breath. She'd procrastinated about coming home as long as possible—an extra hour at the *Oracle* meeting, a long chat with Megan in the parking lot, and a slow, sight-seeing drive back home. Now the plan was simple: jog straight to the room and get into productive "good daughter" mode.

Elizabeth turned the knob, took a quick scan into the living room . . . and stopped. Both parents and Jessica were sitting on the couch, looking up at Elizabeth as if she had skipped curfew again.

"There you are!" Mr. Wakefield said. "We've been waiting for you, Liz. Come on in and let's have a little talk."

*A little talk . . . Why is he so chipper about this?*

Elizabeth tossed her book bag by the bottom of the stairs and ambled into the living room. The scene made her stomach curl with anxiety. The whole family (minus Steven) was staring at her as if she were a really intriguing museum exhibit. Had she stepped into a parallel universe? She sat down on the couch next to Jessica and tapped her hands on her thighs.

"We've been talking with Jessica, and she's made some very good points about the whole situation the other night," Mrs. Wakefield began, already pacing. Elizabeth snuck a glance at her sister, who winked back. "We've never had an antagonistic relationship with either of you, and we don't want to start now. Our main concern as parents is that you, Jessica, and Steven get all the support, love, and *discipline* that you need to navigate your lives and be happy, successful people."

Where was she going with this? It sounded like she had taken that quote straight out of a book on parenting. Probably not a good time to call her mom out on plagiarism, though.

Mrs. Wakefield stopped behind Mr. Wakefield's chair. She rested her hands on his shoulders, as if to combine forces for this important parental point. "But first and foremost, we want to be good *listeners*." Mrs. Wakefield paused, nodding emphatically. "Do you two feel like you can talk to us . . . about anything?"

Elizabeth looked at Jessica. Everyone knew the

universal truth that there were certain things you just *don't* discuss with your parents. But Elizabeth really didn't have much to hide from them, and Jessica was already nodding, so Elizabeth did the same.

"Well, that's good to hear," Mrs. Wakefield said, tucking her hair behind her ear. "Because you can. We don't want you to shut us out because you're afraid we're going to flip out and ground you."

Elizabeth crossed her arms, confused by her mother's logic. "Mom, it's kind of hard not to be afraid of getting grounded . . . when that's all you've been talking about for the last couple of days."

"I understand that, Elizabeth," Mrs. Wakefield said. "We don't want to have to ground you at all, and we'll try our best not to. But there has to be some sort of punishment for when you or Jessica clearly steps over the line."

Mrs. Wakefield walked away from Mr. Wakefield, apparently deep in thought. Elizabeth watched her moving profile and listened to a lawn mower humming down the block. This family discussion was moving in slow motion, and she just wanted to get the sentencing over with.

"We've all been through a lot of tough changes because of the earthquake, and it's made communication difficult," Mrs. Wakefield continued. "But now that we're back in our own house, things are going to return to normal. We're going to have regular family dinners, some outings and weekend activities, and more talk and support all around."

Elizabeth tried to remember the old "normal" Wakefields. It had been a while. Her mind shuffled through all the turmoil since then—living with two other families, adjusting to a totally changed school, the never-ending Conner McDermott saga—and the thought of the old, stable Wakefield clan sounded so inviting. A warm smile crept onto Elizabeth's face just thinking about it.

"Do you both agree with what I've said?" Mrs. Wakefield said.

Elizabeth looked up—her mother was back at Mr. Wakefield's side, and he wore a genuine, fatherly smile. Elizabeth didn't need Jessica's support for this one.

"Totally," she said. "I can't wait for things to return to normal."

"Do you have anything to add?" Mrs. Wakefield added.

Elizabeth shook her head.

"Okay, then. Enough of that," Mrs. Wakefield said.

End of discussion? Was she actually getting off this easy? Elizabeth decided she should make her move quickly before they thought of something else. She put her hands on her thighs, got up, and exhaled.

"We're not quite done yet, Elizabeth," Mr. Wakefield said, no longer smiling. "There is the matter of your punishment."

*There's that.* Elizabeth sat back down on the edge of the couch and braced her knees.

"I'll make it short and sweet—you've got one month," Mr. Wakefield said, extending his finger. "In that month you have three conditions: You've got to pull up your grades, spend more time working on the *Oracle,* and get a job."

*Check. Check. Check.* Elizabeth had already planned on doing all three as part of her own self-imposed sanity-maintenance program.

"If you agree to those conditions and show us some effort right away . . . then you're officially ungrounded, and you can even go out on this double date with Jessica tonight," Mr. Wakefield said. "How does that sound?"

*Lenient?* Elizabeth looked over at Jessica, who was covering a smile with her hand. She felt her pulse quicken but tried to hold in the excitement. "That sounds fine," Elizabeth said, shrugging. "Thanks for being so understanding. I'll start working on all three of those things right away."

"That's exactly what we wanted to hear," Mr. Wakefield said. He pried himself up from the chair and kissed Mrs. Wakefield on the cheek. "Ooh, look at the time," he continued, checking his watch with mock concern. "You two better get ready for the big date."

Elizabeth felt the muscles in the back of her neck loosen. The tide of her life was definitely shifting toward the positive direction. Her family was in her corner, and she no longer felt like a stranger in her own life. *Good karma, good karma,* she thought, rising from her seat with a smile.

Elizabeth walked toward the hallway phone with conviction. Conner wouldn't be psyched, but it didn't matter. She wouldn't let his negativity bring her down. They were going on a double date tonight— and they were going to have a damn good time.

Because she was more than just "in control" now. For the first time in—maybe her entire life— Elizabeth Wakefield was *free!*

# Jessica Wakefield

Will is good-looking, romantic, attracted to me (and says it), fun, and affectionate, and he can bring me to my knees with a kiss. Pretty much all I could ask for in a guy.

But there's one thing about Will that bothers me: Will is too strong willed. Which wouldn't be a big deal except that I'm pretty strong willed myself, and I refuse to become another Melissa who just follows his orders like a pet. Like today, when he made that reservation for tonight at eight-thirty without asking. It was really sweet . . . but he can't get in the habit of dictating my life and making decisions for me. Maybe I'm being a little too

Lilith Fair here, but I've seen what happens when women give up their "say" early on in a relationship. They take a couple of little pushes, and pretty soon they're getting shoved.

At the same time I don't want to engage in a battle of the wills . . . with a guy named Will.

# CHAPTER 6

## The Future Starts Now

Andy Marsden lay down on his bed and pulled the huge, shiny tome out of its plastic bag. His mom had bought it for him over a year ago, during one of those maternal anxiety attacks she occasionally suffered from. He extended it out in front of him with both hands, blocking out the ceiling light, and read the daunting title to himself—*The Complete Guide to Colleges*.

The weight of the book seemed like a good omen. As heavy as it was, there had to be a college in it for him . . . and just about any other fully functioning human with a high-school degree. Why was that powder-blue-wearing guidance counselor, Mr. Nelson, freaking out like Andy was going to be banned from every college in the country? It wasn't *that* hard to get in.

Andy pulled open the book, relishing the sound of a new book spine cracking and the raw smell of pulpy paper. Where should he start? Hmmm. Maybe he should check out Angel's school, Stanford. Just for kicks. Obviously it would be a reach, Angel having been such a homework-aholic and all. But who knows? It's not like the kid was Einstein.

The colleges were arranged by state, and he saw at the top of the page that he was in Missouri. Its state schools seemed to have every possible combination covered—like Missouri U., Missouri Southern State College, Southwest Missouri State, Northwest Missouri State University, Northeastern Missouri Southwest Tech State, South-East-West-North Missouri Polytechnic Institute, and so on. Then there were the random schools with regal-sounding names like Carleton and Hunter and Colby-Sawyer, probably named after rich people who had founded colleges so that their slacker kids could get degrees.

Andy flipped back to California, and there it was: Stanford University.

"Wow." Andy said it to himself quietly. "Stanford." Just saying the word made him feel smart. There were a couple of pictures of the campus—green lawns, gothic architecture, ivy-covered walls, hot young women with books, smiling for no apparent reason. This Stanford place seemed like a decent spot to spend four years . . . or the rest of his life, for that matter.

*Now let's check out the bad part,* he thought, turning the page. There was a grid in the middle of the page, filled with numbers. *Let's see, here. . . . Average SAT score . . . What? 1412!* Andy sat upright and leaned against his headboard. That was the average? In what solar system? He looked farther down the grid for the average GPA—maybe that was the loophole. But 3.72!

"This is depressing," Andy muttered. "I better check out a school that's not just for superheroes."

Since he was already in the California section, Andy figured he should check out UCLA—a school for mere mortals like himself. He remembered a funny, laid-back guy from last year's senior class, Richard Sosa, who Andy used to skip PE with every once in a while. Richie was a clown, and he was at UCLA now. In fact, the more he thought about it, UCLA seemed like a perfect match—respectable state school in the city, with all kinds of funky people doing interesting stuff. Maybe he would get involved in the film industry, or call Richie, or even join a fraternity and turn into Joe College. Why not?

UCLA—perfect. The pictures of its campus were even more inviting than Stanford's. Same plush lawns and nice buildings but more activity, more fine-looking ladies, and not all that stuffy, calculator-toting, Ivy-coated garbage. He licked his fingers and slowly, hesitantly turned the page to check out the . . . *aaahh!* SATs, 1170 for in-state! GPA, 3.37! Where did they find all these people? Were colleges importing brainpower from overseas? He had always assumed that state schools were there for promising upstarts from within the state who didn't wish to venture far from Mom and Pop.

Andy tried to think of who among his friends could possibly get into colleges with such absurd requirements. Conner didn't count—he was one of those mutants who never seemed to study but aced everything anyway. Elizabeth and Maria didn't count either because they were superambitious, top-of-the-class types. But what about Tia? Where would Tia go to school? She had decent grades and SATs, probably no better than his own. Of course, she did have some extracurriculars—like four years of cheerleading, volleyball, and a bunch of volunteer work. But wait—what about Ken? That guy never studied. *Note to self: Commiserate with Ken sometime about how bleak our futures look.*

Andy looked back down at the evil college bible in his hands. He really shouldn't give up so easily. California had left him out to dry. No big deal. There were a lot of other, friendlier states . . . like in the Midwest. How about one of the *I* states, Indiana or Illinois or Iowa, one of those? He pulled the book open to the middle and landed in the Iowa section. Maybe it was fate.

"Andrew Marsden forged a new life for himself, deep in corn country."

He sat up and turned to what looked like—from the pictures—a respectable school. Grinnell College. He had never heard of it. But at this point that seemed like a good thing. He read the description aloud. "A small, cozy, liberal-arts school with a progressive agenda . . . where students have intimate contact with an excellent staff of professors." That sounded all right. He wasn't exactly sure what it meant, but he figured he was as "cozy" and "progressive" as the next guy.

Now for the moment of truth. Andy had noticed a pattern here: First page, pretty pictures = happy. Second page, scary numbers = depressed. But this was Grinnell, not Harvard. They probably had an extra statistical category for farm experience and 4-H prizes. He licked his index finger, touched it to the upper-right corner of the page, and turned. His eyes immediately shot to the grid in the middle of the page.

"What?" The requirements were even tougher than UCLA's.

Andy slammed the book shut and ran his hand through his tousled red hair. Was this possible? He didn't have an ice cube's chance in the Sahara at getting into Grinnell College . . . and he'd never even heard of the place! Was it known to Iowans, or whatever they called themselves, as the "Ivy of Iowa"? Or was he just an underachiever in a country chock-full of overachievers?

*I need to lie down.* Andy reclined his lanky body on the bed, heart still fluttering wildly. He looked up at his ceiling light, bright and piercing like a lunar eclipse. Was there nowhere to hide? He turned over on his side and stared at the digital blues and reds on the face of the stereo. It was a thought that had never really occurred to him before. But now, stuck in the adrenaline rush of panic, it seemed not only possible but probable. *Andy Marsden's not going to college.*

He pictured those TV commercials he had always joked about for local community colleges—CTT Technical Institute, Valley Tech, and all those. With slogans like, "CTT: Where your dreams are just a diploma away." The commercials always had some regular-looking Joe Schmo looking at blips on the screen of some mechanical device and smiling dimly, like he had finally found his one true skill. Were those guys cracking a thousand on their SATs? What if CTT rejected him too?

A flurry of horrific images shot through Andy's mind. He pictured himself standing at the end of the grocery-store checkout line, stacking a bunch of bananas on a box of Twinkies and waiting for his cigarette break. Standing at attention in his army-reserve uniform, saluting Captain Bitter. Tossing a huge plastic bag onto the back of a smelly garbage truck. Sitting on the couch next to a bowl of cheese puffs, watching his favorite soap opera and listening for the mailman to deliver this month's unemployment check. Andy shook his head, suddenly disgusted with himself. Why was he lying here, watching his life go down the tubes?

Andy grabbed the college book at his side. Until he could look that book square in the eye, he didn't want to see it again. He reached his arm over the side of the bed and tossed the huge book under the frame. One day he would look back on this moment as a turning point in his life. The point where Andy Marsden got fed up and vowed to quit his dead-end career as a slacker. The point where he embarked on a career of discipline. The point where he decided to change his ways and get into college, a good college. *The future starts now,* Andy thought, his satisfied smile leaking into the pillow beneath him.

*Right after I take a quick power nap.*

"Could you pass me that atomic green stuff?" Conner said, motioning to the little bottle of hot sauce across the table. He was less interested in the sauce than in catching Elizabeth's attention to see whether he wasn't the only one struggling with this painfully dull conversation. It had gone from football to football, with a brief stop at cheerleading, and they were already into their entrées.

"Sure," Elizabeth said, grabbing the bottle and placing it in front of him. She flashed a warm smile and brushed her hand across his forearm. He zeroed in on her with his most penetrating gaze, hoping she would catch it. No dice.

Conner reluctantly glanced at Will. "You were saying something about, uh, *football*—"

"Oh, yeah, right," Will broke in, obviously incapable of detecting sarcasm. "It's so cool to see how two totally different schools, with opposite philosophies of football, can come together to form a . . . a . . ." Will searched for the right phrase, waving a nacho around in a circle with his hand. "A finely tuned football machine."

*I'm going to choke myself on a burrito.* Conner nodded, feigning interest. He looked at Jessica, who was nodding in the exact same way. Was she bored too?

"For those of us who don't live for SportsCenter . . . what does that mean?" Elizabeth asked. Conner had to struggle to keep his jaw from dropping. How could she encourage him?

"It's like this," Will said, leaning forward. "El Carro was always a risk-taking team. They had a run-and-gun offense, where they threw the ball for long yardage every two or three downs. On defense their linebackers were real aggressive and they blitzed a lot."

"That's fascinating," Conner said, eliciting a slit-eyed look from Elizabeth. Will didn't even blink.

"But Sweet Valley has always been a more conservative, old-school-football kind of squad," he continued. "You know, a lot of running plays up the middle. . . ."

Conner was dumbfounded. Could Will possibly be that stupid? No way. He must just be ignoring Conner. Which was worse, stupidity or complete self-absorption?

Conner decided he didn't want to think about it and tuned out. He noticed a group of waiters singing some type of Spanish happy-birthday song to a customer in a corner table. He hadn't been to Viva

Zapata's before and was surprised at how cool the place was. It didn't try too hard to be *Mexican*, like other restaurants he had been to—with sombrero-shaped hanging lights and Mexican flags and all that jazz. The wooden booths, dim lighting, and old Mexican artifacts on the wall made the place seem kind of romantic. Which made the situation all the more maddening because he should be here with Elizabeth *alone*. Ever since he'd picked her up, looking scrumptious as usual in one of those sexy wrap-around skirts, he'd known this double-date thing was completely unnecessary. At the very least they wouldn't be talking about football all night. Actually, they probably wouldn't be talking at all. . . .

". . . so it took us a long time to bring the two different styles together and convince all the Sweet Valley guys that Coach Kiernan's style was good," Will continued, his deep voice getting louder as his excitement grew. "But now it's like we've got a double threat. We've got the hard-nosed, disciplined defense of the old Sweet Valley style, and we've also got this more aggressive offense, which allows me to use my arm a little more and throw bombs to our receivers. That's how we surprised Big Mesa—they expected the old running game, and I just kept tossing it over their heads for touchdowns. We looked pretty unstoppable out there, didn't we, Jessica?" Will asked, putting his arm around her.

"I couldn't really tell," Jessica answered, shrugging

86

self-consciously. She caught Conner's eye and seemed to sense his indifference. "I was too busy trying to wake up the crowd."

Will didn't say anything. He just forced a laugh and planted a peck on Jessica's cheek.

*Can someone get me a barf bag?* Conner looked down into his messy clump of steak, beans, rice, and gooey, cheesy vegetables and realized he'd lost his appetite. When had Will become this shallow? Maybe it was part of football tryouts. Coach Kiernan had probably weeded out all players with necks smaller than tree trunks and any interest in life beyond the gridiron.

Conner glanced over at Elizabeth again. She was watching Will whisper into Jessica's ear, her cheeks flush with a happiness that bordered on envy. How could she tolerate this? No, that wasn't the question. *Why am I tolerating this?* It was exactly the type of cutesy nightmare that had kept him out of the dating realm for so long. Was this worth it for a girl—any girl?

Conner turned to Elizabeth. He focused in on the silver chain choker that circled Elizabeth's neck and brushed against her soft tendrils of blond hair. He wanted to touch her there, to slide his fingers around to the back of her neck and push upward, sending chills down her spine. But not here. Not in front of all these innocent onlookers trying to enjoy their burritos. And especially not with Freddie Football mirroring his every move with Elizabeth's twin sister across the table. It was like a scene from a bad made-for-TV movie, *Twin Hearts* or *Double Dare*—something brutal like that.

"So, Conner," Jessica said, snapping him out of his daze. "Are you still playing guitar? I've heard you're a great musician."

"Yeah, I still play some." Conner paused and pressed his tongue into his lower lip. Should he go on? Will's piercing eyes seemed to be sizing him up, as if he were a rival quarterback. "'Great' would be a stretch, though, considering my only audience is Megan doing homework in the next room, who's always on the verge of smashing my guitar into little bits."

"Don't be humble," Jessica added, shaking her head. "Liz has told me about you. And I overheard some sophomore girls hyperventilating over Conner "Swoon-Worthy" McDermott's gig at House of Java a while back. I'd love to hear—"

Will's chair grated against the floor with an irritating squeal. Apparently the conversation had taken an unappealing turn. "I'll be right back. Gotta hit the men's room."

Conner smirked. *More like, gotta hit the ego-inflation chamber.*

"Could we get the check over here?" Will called, waving his hand at the waitress.

Jessica knitted her brow. Couldn't he see she

was still picking at her plate? "What's the rush, Will?" she asked.

He leaned toward her. His freshly shaven scent demanded Jessica's attention. "It's been a nice little group outing here," he said softly. "But let's go someplace more . . . *intimate.*"

"Like where?" Jessica asked, putting down her fork.

"Like to the dam at Olgonquin Lake, where there's some moonlight," he said, smiling.

Jessica felt herself leaning forward. Will's electric blue-gray eyes were so bright, they seemed to be pulling her in like two tractor beams. *Go toward the blue-gray light,* Jessica thought, almost laughing out loud at herself.

"Or we could do something more low-key . . . like watch a movie in my basement," Will added. "I don't care, Jess. I just really want to be alone with you."

Jessica caught Elizabeth's eye. This double date wasn't turning out quite as *double* as she'd planned. "Will, we can't leave them yet."

"Why not?"

"Because we came with them," Jessica whispered. "What would I say? 'Thanks for your company, but Will and I would like to be alone now'? It doesn't work that way."

Will's smile dropped. "I'm sure they want to be alone too. Couples generally do want to be alone at some point in the evening," he said bitterly. "If it makes you feel better, I'll say I'm not feeling well and you're going to come take care of me."

*Great plan. That'll fool 'em.* Jessica leaned her head back in exasperation. How had she gotten caught in another battle of wills? She hated that pushy look of determination on his face, how his eyes went from warm to aggressive in a split second when he saw he might not get his way. *I'm sure it worked on Melissa.* The thought of Melissa succumbing to one of his power plays made Jessica's teeth grind.

"Come on, Jess," Will said, massaging the small of her back. "It's not a big deal—just tell Liz you'll explain later."

"No," Jessica barked, louder than she had planned. She turned toward Will so that his hand slid off her back. "You can push all you want, but you're not going to talk me into this."

"Jessica—"

"I'm not Melissa!"

*Oooh.* That wasn't supposed to come out in actual words. Jessica saw the look of shock on Will's whitened face. Speechless. She looked across the table for support. Elizabeth was paler than pale, and Conner looked like he was about to crack up laughing.

"Here's your check, sir," the waitress said, placing the slip in front of Will. He checked it over quickly.

"I'm leaving." He pulled out a bill and slapped it on the table. "If you want to go on a real date, meet me in the car." Will's chair scraped across the floor, and suddenly he was standing, looking down at her.

90

Jessica saw the hurt in his eyes, but it still felt like a power play. He wasn't getting his way, and he couldn't deal with it. "I'm not coming."

"Fine, then," Will said. "I'm outta here."

Jessica watched incredulously as Will stalked through the restaurant and out the door. It had happened too fast—she wanted to press rewind and run through the whole episode again.

"So," she said, forcing a smile, "you two need a third wheel?"

Conner pulled his car to a stop in the Wakefields' driveway, his hands still tight on the steering wheel. This ranked up there with the most frustrating, worthless evenings he could remember. A potentially enjoyable night with Elizabeth ruined by Testosterone Boy. All too predictable. He should have stayed at home and . . . done absolutely nothing.

Jessica squirmed forward and leaned her head into the front seat. "I'm so sorry tonight didn't . . . end very well," she said.

*Did it begin well?* Conner thought.

Elizabeth patted her sister's forearm reassuringly. "Don't worry about it, Jess. I still had a good time."

"Yeah," Conner lied, staring through the windshield.

"Well, I appreciate you two being cool about it," Jessica said, opening the back door. "Thanks, Conner, for driving me home."

The door slammed, making the car unnaturally

silent. Conner never knew what to say at times like these. It seemed like so much effort to fake that everything was *fine* when he was actually bored and a little miffed.

"So," Conner said, "that was inspiring."

Elizabeth laughed. "Oh, it wasn't that bad. Was it?" She scooted closer to Conner and put her right hand on the steering wheel, caging him in.

"It was pretty brutal, Liz," Conner said, tapping his fingers nervously against the bottom of the steering wheel. "Next time let's just—"

Conner stopped midsentence, sensing Elizabeth's motion. He turned into a rush of perfume and felt Elizabeth's lips brush against his gently, then hover for a moment just millimeters away. She tortured him for a few shallow breaths, then kissed him firmly, pushing his head back against the headrest. A surge of pleasure shot down into his stomach, dissolving all of the night's pent-up tension like salt in boiling water. Just as her passion seemed to be letting up, she slipped her hand behind his neck and pulled him into her. Conner could still feel the kiss coursing through his veins after she had backed away.

"See, it's not so bad," Elizabeth said.

Conner opened his eyes slowly, his face still numb.

"Good," Conner blurted out, too woozy to edit his first thought.

Elizabeth laughed. "Next time it'll just be me and

you—so we can spend more time focusing on . . . the fun stuff."

"Looking forward to it," Conner replied. Overcome by a sudden rush of desire, Conner leaned forward and kissed Elizabeth again. He touched his hand to her cheek gently and actually felt her shiver. When he pulled away, he kissed her nose and then her forehead. Elizabeth kept her eyes closed for a moment, a heady smile playing about her lips.

Elizabeth grabbed her purse and held Conner's eyes a moment. A sincere grin spread across her face, and Conner couldn't help but mirror it.

"I should go," she said finally, breaking the trance. Elizabeth leaned forward and kissed him on the cheek. "Thanks for dinner," she said, wriggling toward the door. "Good night."

"Good night."

Conner exhaled, trying to regain composure. Although there was no reason that a twenty-second kiss should make up for a night of awkward tedium, it did. Conner felt relaxed and content, even . . . happy.

He tilted back his head and sighed.

*What's wrong with me?*

Will Simmons pulled his Blazer to an abrupt stop at the end of his driveway. He turned off the ignition and peered through the storm door into his living room. His mom was watching her prime-time lineup. *What a wasted evening. . . .*

Will pictured the look on Jessica's face before he left the restaurant. Pursed lips, searing blue-green eyes, set jaw, arms folded across her body. He wouldn't have left Jessica there if she hadn't looked so disgusted, as if he were a possessive, wife-beating husband or something. He just wanted to be alone with her, that's all. Why did she have to be so high maintenance? And why did she have to embarrass him in front of Conner McDermott, who probably already thought of him as a mental-midget jock?

Will pounded his fist against the dashboard. He had to stop thinking about this, or something might get broken. He climbed out his door, slammed it, and stomped up the front steps. *Mom better not ask for an evening recap, or I'm gonna lose it,* he thought, opening the door with extra caution.

Mrs. Simmons's head shot up from the television set. "Will?"

"What, Mom?"

"Is something wrong?" Mrs. Simmons asked in a maternal tone. "Why are you home so early? Is Jessica with you?"

Will hated when she did this—three questions in succession, none of which he wanted to answer. "No, Jessica's not with me . . . and I don't want to talk about it," he said, starting up the stairs toward his room.

"Oh, I'm sorry, honey," Mrs. Simmons said, her tone softening. "By the way, Will, Melissa stopped by."

Will stopped midstride on the stairs. "She did?"

"You just missed her," Mrs. Simmons answered. "She dropped something off for you . . . a big box. I left it on your bed."

*Interesting,* Will thought. "Thanks, Mom."

He jogged up the stairs. Had Melissa bought a present to win him back? That would be outright desperation. And yet it would be totally like her. She had probably let the episode with Jessica in the cafeteria courtyard run over and over in her head until she rushed out to the mall and splurged on a nice shirt or some expensive cologne.

He hustled into his bedroom and slammed the door, half psyched and half sickened at the thought of a make-up gift. The box was on the edge of his bed. It was big but unwrapped—didn't look much like a present. He untucked the top flaps and tore into it.

It took Will a moment to process what he was seeing, and then his heart gave an exaggerated thump.

He pulled out his old football jersey—lucky number nine—and laid it on the bed. Underneath there were some CDs, a T-shirt he'd won at a school fair, a pair of boxers he'd let Melissa borrow once. . . .

Will couldn't believe it. Melissa was doing the whole return-all-your-ex's-stuff-to-purge-him-from-your-life thing.

Will felt his stomach contract. Three and a half years of dating Melissa—talking every day, sharing every thought, comforting her constantly—and this was all it meant to her? A box full of returnable memories? She was his first love. He thought they were above all those immature dating rituals, including the you're-out-of-my-life-for-good breakup. Guess not.

Will started sorting through the box again, the pit in his stomach deepening with each meaningless little knickknack. Some pens, a couple of recruiting letters from college football programs, a mix tape. There was a birthday card from Melissa he'd accidentally left at her house. He opened the card and read it.

Dear Will:

You are the world to me. You're the most beautiful person I know, and I feel honored to be your girlfriend. I hope your sixteenth birthday is as sweet as you are. I'll do my best to help out. I'll always love you,

Melissa

Will shut the card and smiled. There was something so touching about Melissa's simplicity. She loved him, and she said it. That was that. And he had loved her back. Not like this prima-donna, don't-tell-me-what-to-do garbage from Jessica. If Melissa weren't so needy . . . Will shoved the card back in its box, unwilling to let his guilt get the best of him. He felt something fuzzy and yanked on it. What? Will pulled out a sweater and held it before him. Melissa had returned the brown cashmere sweater he had bought her for Christmas last year. What was that all about? The sweater belonged to her. There was no reason to give it back.

There was a knock at Will's door.

"Yes?" he asked.

"Will, I just wanted to make sure you were okay," Mrs. Simmons's voice said sweetly. "I know you don't want to talk, but it's not healthy to shut yourself off and let your emotions get the best of you."

"Come in, Mom," Will said, rolling his eyes.

Mrs. Simmons opened the door slowly, pushing her blond curls behind her ears like a nervous child. "How are you feeling?"

"Fine," he said. "Mom, what was Melissa like when she came over? Did she seem sad or depressed, or was she acting weird in any way?"

Mrs. Simmons narrowed her eyes slightly. "No, not at all. In fact, I thought she seemed unusually cheerful . . . considering the situation between you two. We chatted a little while about cheerleading and school and her college search, and then she left."

*Unusually cheerful?* Melissa had put their relationship in a box, dropped it off at his house, and she was *cheerful?* She should have been a total wreck. Maybe Melissa had gone over the edge. Like those

97

freaky, schizophrenic people in movies who always had big, plastic smiles on their faces despite the three bodies in the trunk of the car.

"So she didn't ask how I was doing or anything?" Will asked.

"No," Mrs. Simmons answered matter-of-factly, "she just told me to give you that box."

"Okay. Thanks, Mom," Will said. "Don't worry about me. I'm just . . . having a bad day."

"I'm sorry, hon," Mrs. Simmons said, placing one hand on the doorknob. "Are you worried about Melissa? Did she leave a note in that package or something?"

*Good point.* It wasn't like Melissa to not leave a note.

"No," Will answered. "Actually, it sounds like she's doing just fine."

"Good. I'll be downstairs if you need me." Mrs. Simmons smiled and walked out.

Will turned and checked out the pile of goodies on his bed. What was Melissa doing? She always had a plan, a strategy. Will considered the facts. Melissa returned all his stuff, including the sweater. She was happy and nonchalant with his mom. And she didn't leave a note. Will was reluctant to believe it, but the facts all pointed to one conclusion.

Melissa was finally over him.

# Will Simmons

I remember the advice Angel Desmond gave me when I was torn between Melissa and Jessica a while back: "Dump the manipulative ball and chain and go for the blonde." A wise man speaks.

The more I think about it, I'm so glad I took his advice. I mean, Jessica's a handful, and I'm still pretty irritated with her for tonight's little fiasco. But she's still beautiful and exciting and fun, and she's definitely a <u>challenge.</u> Not to mention, as difficult as Jessica is, she'll never be the nonstop emotional roller-coaster ride that Melissa was. All that drama. The nonstop issues. The petty little jealousies. And now,

after all that we've been through,
after three and a half years together,
Melissa actually had the nerve to
drop that stupid box off. Thank
God that woman's out of my life.

Now if I could just get her out of
my <u>head.</u>

# CHAPTER 7

# Throwing Symbolic Enchiladas

Jessica rolled over and laid her head on the other pillow. It was cooler, softer—overall the better pillow. Maybe she would finally be able to go back to sleep.

She patted her head into it a couple of times like a kitten trying to form the perfect comfort spot. She slowed down her breathing and tried to relax. *Think of floating on a cloud.* . . . "This is ridiculous," Jessica said to herself, sitting upright in bed. Her mind was racing, and she just flat out couldn't relax. She had to deal with this Will thing.

All last night, as she tried to distract herself with reruns and ice cream and, finally, *homework,* she'd been thinking about their standoff at the restaurant. She even had a dream about it, where she dumped her enchilada on Will's lap and felt like an idiot afterward. What did that mean? Was her subconscious telling her to "dump" Will? That seemed like a drastic interpretation. Jessica remembered from a book she'd read about dreams that they often reflected tensions and thoughts and guilt left over from "day residue." *Guilt.* That was the problem. But it's not like she had *actually* dumped a steaming enchilada on Will, so what was all this guilt about?

Jessica heard her stomach gurgling and twisting around, like it had all last night. She'd tried to quiet it with a half bucket of coffee Häagen-Dazs before she realized it wasn't a hunger issue. It was stress— an aching, perpetually empty stomach, like what she had felt when Melissa had spread all those rumors. *Wait a second. . . .*

"I'm not Melissa." Jessica said it out loud.

Jessica threw off the covers. That was the comment she felt really guilty about, the symbolic enchilada she'd thrown at Will in her dream. And she should feel guilty about it. It was okay to stand her ground and not give in to Will's pressure, to not dis Elizabeth and Conner on a double date. But she had no right to even bring up Melissa, let alone put her down and imply that she had been Will's puppy-dog girlfriend.

Jessica looked at the clock—nine-nineteen. Was it psycho to call him this early on a Saturday morning? She reached toward the phone, then pulled back her hand.

Maybe she should just forget about it and never mention it again. She would just be really cool and low maintenance and . . . no, that was so immature. She needed to swallow her pride.

"Aaahhh!" Jessica stage-whispered a scream.

She picked up the phone and speed-dialed Will's

number before she could change her mind. Her head bobbed back and forth nervously as the phone rang— once, twice, three times. Jessica started to rehearse a short, sweet apology for the answering machine.

But on the fourth ring someone picked up.

"Hello." The husky voice was unmistakable.

"Hi, Will," Jessica said, sounding as guilty as she felt.

"Hey, Jess," Will mumbled.

Jessica paused awkwardly, wondering whether she should even attempt small talk. She felt her stomach flip-flop again. "Will, I'm really sorry about the whole enchilada thing. . . ."

"What are you talking about?" Will cut in.

Jessica took a deep breath and started again. "What I meant was, I'm really sorry about last night."

"It's all right," Will said. Totally unconvincing.

"No, it's not," Jessica blurted out. "I should have never brought up Melissa. You two went out for a long time, and I had no right to insult her like that."

"That's—"

Jessica didn't let him finish. "I didn't mean to put her down or imply that she followed you around like a . . ." Jessica hesitated. "I won't bring Melissa up again, I promise."

"I don't understand why you brought her up anyway," Will said, his anger seeping through. "It wasn't about Melissa—it was about us spending some time alone . . . for once."

"I know, you're right," Jessica said. "You just

wanted to be alone with me. I just thought you were being a little pushy, that's all."

"Maybe—"

"I want to be alone with you too, Will."

There was a pause, then a sigh. "You say that, Jess, but then it doesn't happen," Will said. "I'm beginning to think you're afraid of me."

Jessica's face felt hot. Was that some sort of challenge? "What are you doing this afternoon?" she asked, determined. "We could watch a movie in your basement, like you mentioned last night."

"I've got . . ." Will trailed off. "I promised my mom I'd run a bunch of errands for her."

"Well, how about tonight?" Jessica asked, twisting the phone cord around her finger until it almost cut off her circulation.

"You want to try again tonight?" Will asked.

"Sure," Jessica said.

"All right," Will said flatly. "I'll pick you up around eight. Is that okay?"

"That's perfect," Jessica shot back enthusiastically. "I'm psyched."

"Good, I'll see you at eight, then," Will said. "But I really should go now—I promised my mom."

"No problem," Jessica said, trying to sound as low maintenance as possible.

"Bye, Jess."

"Bye."

Jessica hung up the phone and bit her fingernail.

There was something in Will's voice—a seed of doubt—that came through and killed some of her confidence. She would have to stomp out that seed of doubt tonight before it grew into a big, ugly tree.

Conner McDermott looked down at the frayed string hanging off his guitar. *Second one this week,* he thought. Maybe broken guitar strings were a sign from above that he should snap out of hermit mode and actually leave his room. Or maybe it just meant he should restring his guitar.

Conner reached for his guitar case on the floor but jolted upright at the sound of a ringing phone. *Liz.* It had to be—his guy friends would never call this early. *Let the answering machine deal with my boyfriend duties.* Conner ground his teeth in irritation. Why had he even thought of the word *boyfriend?*

The phone rang again. It sounded louder this time, as if it felt neglected. Conner looked at it—a black cordless phone standing upright in its holster, antenna pointed at the ceiling. It seemed to be looking back at him, like a little creature. "Talk to your girlfriend, you wuss!" it cried with each ring. "You know you want to!"

The phone cried again. One more ring might drive him insane. So he shot up off the bed and grabbed it.

"Hello," Conner said.

"Well, hello," an older man's voice said enthusiastically. "May I please speak to a Mr. Conner McDermott?"

The voice sounded official. Definitely not a friend—probably a telemarketer. Conner decided not to hang up, just in case he'd won something.

"This is Conner McDermott."

"Mr. McDermott, this is your lucky day," the man said, pausing for a response.

Conner assumed he should act surprised. "Oh, really?"

"That's right," the man continued in a hurried, mover-and-shaker's tone. "My name is Roland Eversworth, and I'm a talent scout for Hollywood Records. My cousin Arnold attended your solo gig at a local coffee joint, House of Jabba or something, and he recorded a couple of your songs on his minirecorder. Arnold was so impressed with your act that he sent the tape to my office. The long and short of it is—I think you've got real talent, Mr. McDermott."

Conner narrowed his eyes. "Who is this?"

"There's more," the voice answered confidently. "Hollywood would like to offer you a—" His voice broke off, and Conner heard a little snicker in the background. "We'd like to offer you a four-year, six-million-dollar—" The voice broke off again, this time into a loud cackle.

Conner recognized the cackle and smiled into the phone. "Evan, you're such a punk."

"What's up, McD.?" Evan said, still laughing. "Thought you might fall for that bit—I've been working on my Mr. Bigwig accent."

"What are you doing up so early?" Conner asked.

"I wanted to catch you early, before you went into hiding," Evan said. "You got plans for tonight?"

Conner picked up a dart from his desk and casually flung it at the board on his closet door.

"No."

"Good, because Reese and Tommy told me about this Big Mesa party tonight, and apparently we're on the VIP list."

"Sounds cool," Conner said. Reese Taylor and Tommy Puett were two of Conner's friends from El Carro who had ended up at Big Mesa after the earthquake. Conner wasn't exactly the keep-in-touch type, so he hadn't seen them in weeks.

"So you're in?" Evan asked.

"Most definitely."

"That's what we like to hear, McD. I'll send out an all-points bulletin to all eligible bachelorettes," Evan continued. "It's at 33 Rivington Court."

"All right, man," Conner said. "See you later."

"Cool. Later on."

Conner clicked off the phone. He thought about some of the El Carro people who would be at this party. Besides Evan, Reese, and Tommy there weren't many he wanted to see, really. And the prospect of scoping women seemed strangely foreign. Still, it would be good to not have to think about Elizabeth for a night, to distance himself a little and just . . . check out the scene. Maybe some "eligible bachelorette" would step up to the plate and make him completely forget about her. Doubtful, but maybe.

The phone rang again. *Speak of the devil.* If it was Elizabeth, he just wouldn't mention the party. That wasn't lying—it was more like withholding the truth.

Conner clicked on the phone. "Hello?"

"Hello, may I please speak to Conner?" It was Elizabeth's voice.

Conner wanted to feel suffocated, but it was hard. Elizabeth's voice was so sweet and airy that he felt his mood lift another notch.

"I'm sorry," he said. "Conner's not accepting calls right now. Would you like to leave a message with Frieda, his secretary?"

Elizabeth laughed. "Yeah, tell Frieda she better not touch my man or I'll come over and kung fu her miniskirted butt."

Conner smirked. "Easy there," he said, returning to his regular voice. "What's going on?"

"Not much," Elizabeth said. "I was just calling to see what you were up to tonight."

Conner clenched his teeth. *Don't say it. Change the topic.* "Oh, tonight . . ." Conner paused, but he couldn't think of anything. The silence filled him with an inexplicable panic. "Actually, Evan just called about a party out at Rivington Lake." *Shut up, you idiot! Shut up!* "A little get-together with a bunch of El Carro people."

"Oh," Elizabeth said softly. Conner could hear

the hurt in her voice. His heart was racing, and he had no idea why.

"You're welcome to come," he blurted out involuntarily. *What the hell is wrong with me?* "I mean, you won't know anyone, so it might be a little annoying."

"I don't care," Elizabeth said. "It might be cool to meet some of your other friends."

"The only thing—"

"Hey, Conner, I think that's Tia calling me back on the other line," Elizabeth said, her voice rushed. "Do you want to wait a second?"

"If it's Tia, I could be waiting awhile," Conner said. "I'll pass."

"All right," Elizabeth said. "I'll see you tonight, then, at . . ."

"Around nine," Conner said reluctantly. "Tell Tia I said hey."

"Okay. Bye."

"Bye."

Conner clicked off the phone. He threw it against his pillow and looked up at the ceiling. Had he lost all self-control? Had he lost his mind? Was he really turning into a . . . a boyf—?

He'd rather not say it.


"I'm sick of sitting around like an old widow," Tia announced, slamming her coffee mug on the table. "I feel like I've been wearing a veil around ever since he left for Stanford."

Andy looked into Tia's fiery brown eyes. She was so inspiring when she got like this—all huffy and determined. When she had phoned in an emergency "venting session" at House of Java earlier that morning, Andy knew exactly what the topic of conversation would be. Angel. Or, should he say, the lack thereof.

"I've written that boy so many e-mails, his in box is probably jammed," Tia said.

"You should—"

"I've sent him care packages, prayers, kisses, and a hundred telepathic messages," Tia added. "But as far as I know, he doesn't get any of them. And regardless, it's just not the same as having him around."

*I don't know if I want to get into this.* Andy looked around, soaking in House of Java's early Saturday ambience. Only a couple of other tables were occupied. He recognized the bearded guy in the dark corner booth as HOJ's resident intellectual—unshaven, with frazzled, curly hair that stuck out like an Afro and skin tinted the unhealthy hue of milky coffee. A couple of tables away from him was a generation-X couple—tattooed but respectable looking—sipping at steamy drinks and chatting energetically. A shock of morning sunlight blanketed the couple so thoroughly that they both wore sunglasses to cope with it.

"You're not even listening, Andy!" Tia half shouted.

"Yes, I am," Andy joked. "You were saying something about Angel."

"Good guess, you dork," Tia said.

"Something about how you need his body and soul right here with you," Andy added, prodding her.

"Exactly. If I can't have him here, I at least need to hear from him. We promised that we'd keep in touch somehow—every day."

Andy's eyes glazed. Tia and her rant were slipping off into another direction.

"Hey!" Andy said suddenly. "Snap out of it! I can't handle watching my pillar of strength for the last four years go and lose her mind right when I need her most."

Tia took a sip of her coffee and fixed her eyes intensely on Andy, as if he had spoken The Truth. "You're right," she said, nodding.

*She's losing it,* Andy thought.

"From now on," Tia resolved out loud, "I'm going to keep Angel in a totally separate bracket from the rest of my life."

"You go, girlfriend!" Andy said. He felt obliged to egg her on whenever she got this way.

"I'll keep working hard in school," Tia said. Andy nodded in agreement. "But I'm not gonna get so caught up in work and Angel . . . that I don't live a little. I've got to *play* hard too."

Andy squinted at her. What was that supposed to mean?

"No, no," she said, backing away. "I mean, nothing drastic. I just want to have a little fun before my high-school days have passed me by."

Andy rested his hand on his chin. He remembered his panic attack about not getting into college, about his career as a sanitary engineer. "Not me," he said. "As of this weekend, my playing days are over."

"What are you talking about?" Tia asked.

"I'm saying it's time to deal," Andy answered. "In school and after school, weekends and weekdays, twenty-four/seven, nonstop work mode."

Tia cracked a smile. "No offense, Andy . . . but isn't it a little late for this not-so-new-year's resolution?"

"It's never too late," Andy quipped. He pointed at his coffee mug confidently. "I'm only drinking this mochaccino right here to get ready for a full day of studying."

"Is that right?" Tia prodded.

"Damn skippy," Andy said.

"What does that even mean?" Tia asked with a laugh.

"I don't know. It just came out," Andy said. "Think I could get a scholarship for coining catchy phrases?"

"Not even."

"Well, I'm not even going to that Big Mesa bash tonight," Andy said. "I'll have a little party with my books instead."

Tia exploded with laughter, almost spitting out a mouthful of coffee.

"What's so funny about that?" Andy asked. "You don't think I can study on a Saturday night?"

Tia wiped the coffee off her chin and took a deep

breath. "Um . . . no," she said, still trying to hold back the laughter.

"You just watch," Andy scoffed at her, a little angry at her insensitivity. He didn't need any outside doubt to add to his own huge pile of *self*-doubt. If he had to sit through Tia's woe-is-me, my-Angel's-gone pity fest, she should at least support him in his pursuit of academic competence.

"I'm serious about this, Tia," Andy started up again, uncrossing his legs nervously. "I'm a new hombre. I'm even joining SADD next week. I already talked to the president. And I might do track in the spring."

"Do they need a manager?" Tia joked.

"That's not cool," Andy shot back. What was her problem?

Tia scooted back her chair. "I'm sorry, Andy," she said, reaching over the table to give him a hug. "I have the utmost faith in you. If you really put your mind to it, you could be a starting linebacker on the football team."

"No, I couldn't," Andy quipped.

"All right, you probably couldn't," Tia conceded, sitting back down. "But you can do all those other things you mentioned. Study on a Saturday night, bring up your grades, start extracurricular activities, all that stuff. But you can't just talk about it—you've got to actually do it."

"You're right," Andy agreed. He looked over at Coffeehouse Philosopher Guy, hunched over a well-worn book in the corner, reading intensely. Why couldn't he do that? He looked back at Tia with magnified intensity. If he didn't get out of this coffee pit right now and go hit the books, he might never deal with anything. And people like Tia—his best friends—would always make cute, unfunny jokes about it.

"What is that look for?" Tia asked.

Andy popped up from his seat. "I'm sorry, Tia, but it's time for the new Andy to step up to the plate." He grabbed his jacket off the back of his chair. "I have to get to work . . . right now."

Will Simmons fiddled with the gearshift. He was only a couple of blocks away from Melissa's house, and the familiar scenery—the Exxon gas station on the left, the huge apple tree on the right—had triggered a rush of nervous excitement. Not that this was a big deal. He was just going to stop by Melissa's house and drop off in her mailbox the cashmere sweater she had wrongly returned. Stop, drop, and leave.

The light changed, and Will punched his Blazer into first gear. His eyes darted quickly from side to side. Melissa could be out running on a sunny Saturday like this.

Will drove down Melissa's street slowly, as if tiptoeing. He looked at her next-door neighbor's lawn and remembered the time he had fake-tackled

Melissa onto it while they were walking home one night. They had kissed awhile, wrestling around and laughing, then lain on their backs in the freshly cut grass and talked about the future. How he would be captain of the football team and go on to get a scholarship to some California school nearby. How she would be cheerleading captain and go to the same school. It seemed like a decade ago.

Will pulled his Blazer to a stop at Melissa's mailbox and opened his window. *Stop, drop, and leave.*

"Will, is that you?"

Will craned his neck. Behind him, partly obscured by the side of her house, was Melissa. She was lying out on one of those fold-out sun chairs . . . in a bikini. He instinctively jerked his head away. Could he just shout hello, drop the sweater in the mailbox, and drive off? No. That would be immature, bordering on mean. Will gave Melissa a little half wave, pulled into her driveway, grabbed the plastic bag in the shotgun seat, and got out.

"What's up?" Will said blandly, walking toward her.

"Just catching some rays," Melissa said, sitting upright in the fold-out chair. "What brings you out here?"

Will stopped a couple of yards away from her and put his hands on his hips. Melissa was wearing a yellow string bikini with little blue flowers all over it, and she looked unbelievable. Brown hair brushing against bronze, feminine shoulders. Black,

Audrey-Hepburn-ish sunglasses. He latched his arm behind his neck and tried to look away.

"Will?" Melissa prompted, lifting her glasses to look him in the eyes.

"I'm sorry," Will sputtered. "I just came to bring this back to you." He pulled the cashmere sweater out of its plastic bag and watched Melissa's face for some kind of emotional reaction. Stone cold. Why was she so composed?

"Thanks," Melissa said. "I hope you don't think it was rude of me to bring all that stuff over yesterday. I was just cleaning my room and—"

"I didn't think it was rude," Will said matter-of-factly. He shifted his weight to the other foot. "But you didn't have to return the sweater, Liss. It was a gift, remember?"

Melissa smiled. "I'm sorry," she said. "But I'm happy to have it back—it's such a beautiful sweater."

Will walked toward her with the sweater, keeping his breath steady. *Don't let her get to you.* The co-conut oil hit his nostrils at the same moment her finger brushed his.

"It's good to see you," Will said lamely. He felt like he should say something more intimate, more *real* to her. Like the truth: *I couldn't stop thinking about you last night, Melissa.* Something to show that he hadn't just forgotten her.

Melissa swung her legs over the side of the chair. "Yeah, it's good to see you too, Will," she said, standing up. "I've got to get inside before I burn to a crisp."

Will watched in disbelief as Melissa picked her towel off the chair. Was she actually going to walk away?

"Take care, Will," she said, "and thanks for the sweater."

Will could neither move nor speak. He just nodded.

Melissa gave him a little finger wave. "Bye."

He watched Melissa tiptoe across the driveway, balancing herself playfully with outstretched arms. By the time she reached the far side, Will had come to grips with two cold, hard truths. First of all, Melissa was definitely walking away.

And second, she wasn't coming back.

# TIA RAMIREZ AND ANGEL DESMOND

Tee:    Angel . . . you there?

Angel:  I'm here, baby.

Tee:    How's that Af-Am conference been
        treating you?

Angel:  It's unbelievable, Tia. I don't even
        know where to start. There's just so
        many interesting people. Daughters of
        African diplomats, reggae musicians,
        writers, wanna-be politicians, comedi-
        ans (or people funny enough to be come-
        dians). Incredible people. I've never
        felt so stimulated in my entire life.

Tee:    That's awesome.

Angel:  You're going to love college so much.
        It's just a bunch of smart, hungry young
        people exchanging ideas and just . . .
        hanging out. My roommates are all cool.
        Our common room has become the hangout
        spot for our entire dorm floor. One of
        my roommates, Isaiah, is a DJ, and he's
        been spinning records like every other
        night, and the girls next door always
        come over to hang out and listen. Then
        there's this Russian dude who's basi-
        cally a math genius. The whole thing is
        just mind-blowing.

Tee:    Angel?

Angel: What's up, Tee?

Tee: Did you get a package in the mail?

Angel: I don't think so. Did you send me something?

Tee: Maybe.

Angel: Oh, yeah? You're the best, Tee. I'll keep a lookout for it. By the way, how you doing?

Tee: I'm all right. You know how life is around here. Same old thing . . . minus my favorite boy. Andy has decided to imitate you and become a scholar/athlete/student activist all of a sudden. Very funny.

Angel: That is funny. Tell him I said what's up. I'm really sorry, Tee, but I gotta take off now. I've got to get ready for this dinner and dance tonight. Af-Am activists from five colleges will be there. Isaiah's going to DJ at the dance.

Tee: All right. You have fun . . . but not too much fun. I miss you, Angel.

Angel: I miss you too. Take care. I'll be thinking about you. Love you, Tee. Bye.

      [Angel has signed off]

Tee: I love you too.

# CHAPTER 8

## *The Marsden Theorem*

Will walked up to the mirror and did a full face scan. There was nothing a good shave wouldn't fix.

He shook the can of shaving cream, sprayed a big dollop of white foam into his hand, and covered the lower half of his face with it. As the razor cut its first swath over his stubbly cheek, he tried to visualize tonight's date with Jessica.

It was a habit he'd gotten into when he first started going out with Melissa. He would picture a date going perfectly from beginning to end while he shaved, and then it would run like clockwork. Just like visualizing the perfect pass in football. See the receiver running down the sideline, feel the arm cock and throw with one smooth motion, then see it hit the guy right on the numbers. Boom—touchdown.

Will turned his head and trimmed the bottom of his left sideburn. He imagined himself walking up the driveway, a red rose hidden behind his back, with the light scent of aftershave on his collar. He would ring the front door, take a couple of deep breaths to maintain composure, and wait for Melissa to . . .

"Ouch!"

Will checked out the side of his jaw where a little spot of blood had welled up. He splashed some water on it and tried to regain his concentration. *Jessica's front door.* He focused harder, almost straining his face, until he realized . . . he couldn't picture Jessica's front door. It was Melissa's front door he had been thinking about. Maybe it was because he had just been to her house earlier today. But at the moment the only driveway, the only door, the only *body* he could see in his mind's eye . . . was Melissa's.

Will put down the razor for a second and looked at his reflection. He closed his eyes and tried to imagine any aspect of Jessica's house—totally blank. He tried to envision Jessica's face instead. The picture developed slowly, like an Instamatic Polaroid—the aqua eyes, the dusty blond, chin-length hair, the lips.

Will opened his eyes and picked up the razor, his confidence restored. He didn't have to visualize every single moment of the date. He just had to be able to think of Jessica at a restaurant, any generic restaurant. Pulling out her chair for her, gazing across the table into her eyes, and smiling . . . Will was shaving away now—he had the old rhythm back.

Suddenly, like a flashback, a picture of Melissa shot into his brain. A vivid image of her in the lawn chair, wearing the yellow bikini, lifting off her glasses and smiling. He tried to push it away, but Melissa's image was too concrete.

121

And he had the feeling it wouldn't fade anytime soon.

Andy sat at his bedroom desk, hunched over his calculus book. He was a picture of perfect studying form. Highlighter held tight in his right hand, soft jazz playing on the stereo, and the desk light tilted at exactly the right angle to illuminate the jumble of numbers and equations in front of him.

$y = mx + b$, where $m$ is the slope of the curve at any point.

*Who cares about the slope of the curve?* Andy thought. He'd been asking that type of question for years. Back in the days of multiplication times tables, it was: *Why do we have to multiply so fast? We'll never beat the calculators.* Then in the days of fractions, it was: *Why do we have to learn about numbers that are smaller than one? No one cares about pennies, but at least they're worth one cent.* In geometry Andy had even written down the Marsden theorem. He searched his memory for it. Ah, yes.

Marsden theorem:

If you don't care about $a$ and you don't care about $b$, and $a + b = c$, then you *definitely* will not care about $c$.

Unfortunately Mr. Rowntree had seen the Marsden theorem written on the back of Andy's notebook and gave him an hour of detention as a reward for his breakthrough. That pretty much summed up Andy's math career.

*Get back to work.* Andy started highlighting a passage that looked important, with a bunch of boldface terms about calculating derivatives. He tapped his highlighter against the desk to the beat of jazz snare drums.

Out of the corner of his eye Andy noticed a glimmer of light. He glanced at his closet. There was a shiny object right near his sneakers. Andy decided to investigate since it was time for a little study break anyway.

*No way!* It was his old Game Boy! When he'd lost it a couple of years back, Andy had been so grief stricken that he'd felt like holding a funeral service.

Andy stood up and caressed the video game. *Wonder if I've still got the old skills.* Not that he could really find out since those batteries had probably been dead for months. Might as well try. He pressed the power button, and Tetris, his favorite game, came up on the screen. Unbelievable. He had to play one game, for old times' sake.

Andy chose "one player" and listened to the little Tetris theme song. Ah, what sweet memories! Hundreds of hours—a significant part of his adolescence—spent frantically maneuvering his thumbs and racking up points.

The little Tetris bricks started falling from the sky. Andy guided each one effortlessly into the right spot, turning them sideways and flipping them over, whatever it took. *Still got the magic touch.* Why was knowing calculus more important than knowing how to play Tetris? They both seemed worthless, but at least Tetris was fun.

Andy heard a knock at the door and felt a rush of panic. He wanted to hide the Game Boy, but he was having such a great game. When Mrs. Marsden walked in, he pressed the Game Boy against his chest and stared at her with wild eyes.

"Hey, Mom," Andy said nervously. He turned and walked back toward his desk, slipping the Game Boy into his pocket.

"Working hard, huh?" Mrs. Marsden asked. "Where'd you find your Game Boy anyway?"

*How does she do that?*

"I saw it in the closet there and decided to take a little break," Andy said.

Mrs. Marsden tilted her head. "I don't want to sound preachy here, Andy, but if you're gonna change your studying habits, you can't get distracted by every little beep and flashing light and thought that hits you."

"I know, I know," Andy said, sighing. "I'm trying really hard here."

"I don't mean to discourage you," Andy's mother said with a sympathetic smile. "I know you're trying hard."

Andy sat back down at his desk and picked up his highlighter, hoping his mom would take the hint.

"I'll let you get back to your work now," she said.

Andy heard the door click shut. He pulled the Game Boy out of his pocket and threw it on his bed. No more games. He started reading intensely, processing each word as it came, trying to picture it all in his head. It was all about curves and changing slopes. Anything that he could picture or vaguely understand got the highlighter. It wasn't much.

A loud ring caused Andy to highlight a diagonal streak across the page. The phone. He leaned over and picked it up, happy for another distraction.

"Hello?"

"Andy, it's me."

"Hey, Tee."

"Sorry to bother you while you're studying, but I just couldn't handle being alone any longer. I feel like I'm losing my mind."

"Why?" Andy asked.

"It's just, I can't deal with this Angel thing any-more," Tia practically whined. "I just chatted with him online, and I feel like he lives on another planet. I don't have anything in common with him now . . . and he's not even getting my care packages . . . and then at the end of our chat he said 'love you' instead of 'I love you,' and you know what that means."

"Settle down, Tia," Andy said calmly. "You sound like you're about to have a stroke."

"I can't settle down!" Tia barked.

Andy looked at the phone like *it* was going

crazy. "Isn't there something you can do to take your mind off it?"

"That's what I was kind of calling to ask about," Tia admitted. "I know you're on a new diligent kick and all, but . . ."

"Uh-oh."

"Do you want to go to that party tonight?" Tia blurted out.

Andy squeezed his eyes closed. Why was she doing this to him? She knew how torturous it was.

"Pleeease?" Tia begged.

"Bark like a dog," Andy commanded.

"Give me a break." Tia laughed.

"All right," Andy said with a sigh. "I'll pick you up later."

After Andy hung up the phone, he stared at the jumble of letters and numbers on the page in front of him, then glanced at his bed. In one swift motion he launched out of his chair, grabbed the Game Boy, and landed on his mattress.

There was no real point in getting all involved in calculus if he was just going to have to stop again anyway.

"Thank you," Jessica said as Will pulled out her chair for her. She tucked her silk skirt underneath her and sat down. Will pushed the chair in slowly and affectionately caressed her shoulder.

*Nice to see you again, Dr. Jekyll,* Jessica thought as

Will walked around to his seat. It was amazing how quickly he had transformed from a pushy guy into a perfect gentleman. When he picked her up, Will had pulled a single red rose from behind his back, smiled, and kissed her tenderly on the lips. A great start for a "make-up" date.

Will sat down across from her and pushed the flower vase in the middle of the table to the side. He leaned forward and placed his calloused hands on the table in front of Jessica. She rested hers on top of his and smiled.

"What do you think of this place?" Will asked.

"I love it," Jessica answered. She had heard Lila coo about this restaurant being the hippest, most authentically Italian place in town. The wait staff were olive-skinned Mediterranean types with all-black outfits. There was a huge brick-oven stove in the back and dark, redbrick walls, and one wall was decorated like a Sicilian balcony—with windows, draping flowers, and a fake laundry line.

"Ciao!"

Jessica looked up and saw a slim young waitress with jet-black hair and a huge smile.

"Welcome to Caffé Antica Roma," she said, laying menus in front of them. "I am Rosalina, and I'll be your server this evening. Our specials tonight are the tortellini *alla panna* and the *cavatelli* Bolognese; we have a special soup du jour, the pasta *fagioli*, which is . . ." Rosalina licked her lips and shimmied a little to get her point across. Jessica looked at Will and laughed. "And if you like seafood, we have a calamari marinara over linguini that is out of this world. Would you like to start out with some drinks?"

"I just want a Coke," Will said.

"Diet Coke for me, please," Jessica added.

"No problem," Rosalina said, and walked off.

"So, is Liz totally out of the doghouse with your parents now?" Will asked.

"It looks that way," Jessica said. "She earned points by working all morning with Dad on her college applications. And when I left, she was studying in the living room so they could see her. Mom and Dad eat up that kind of stuff."

"So what about you?" Will said. "Have you thought much about where you're going to apply?"

Jessica tucked her hair behind her ear. "I don't know," she said. "Arizona, maybe. University of Colorado—that campus looks so beautiful. I mean, I'd love to get into UCLA. It's such a good school, and it'd be cool to be in Los Angeles, but I don't know if my grades are good enough."

"No, I don't see you as a UCLA girl," Will said matter-of-factly. "That place is too big and impersonal for you, Jess. You should apply to some smaller schools, where you can really make an impact and maybe even keep cheerleading."

*What's that supposed to mean?* Was she too

small-time for UCLA? Jessica decided not to dignify his suggestion with a response.

"And if you're worried about SATs, you should really prepare," Will continued. He leaned into the table and clasped his hands.

"Oh, yeah?" Jessica asked lukewarmly. Was he going to tell her what to do . . . again? And who had said anything about SATs? She'd taken them last spring and had even scored higher than Elizabeth.

"Absolutely," he said. "I found this great SAT preparation course that meets twice a week after school. They guarantee your score will go up a hundred points. It really works. I'm going to go sign up on Tuesday. I'll just sign you up—"

"You two ready to order yet?" the waitress interrupted, placing a Coke next to Will.

Will looked up at her, obviously annoyed by the intrusion. "Why don't you just get us two of the specials?" he said flippantly. "The tortellini and that calamari seafood dish . . . and maybe some soup too. You want soup, Jess?"

*I haven't even looked at the menu.* Jessica just looked at him and then up at Rosalina. She shot a half smile back. As in, half embarrassment, half sympathy.

"Yeah, give us two soups too," Will said impatiently. He grabbed his own menu, then Jessica's, and handed them both to the waitress.

"Sure," Rosalina said as she walked off.

Will took a sip of his Coke and looked at

Jessica nonchalantly. "So where was I? Oh, yeah, so I could just sign you up for this SAT prep course when I go in on Tuesday—"

"What was *that*?" Jessica asked, stopping him cold.

Will cocked back his head. "What was *what*?"

Jessica raked her fingers through her hair. "You just ordered for me without even asking what I wanted. And you treated that waitress like your personal servant. No thanks, no please, not even a smile."

"Oh, come on, Jess," Will answered, throwing up his hands. "First of all, the woman interrupted me. Second, neither of us has even looked at the menu yet and she's rushing us to order—so we might as well get the specials she recommended. Doesn't that make sense?"

Jessica felt heat rise to her head, making her dizzy with anger. Could Will actually be this clueless and insensitive? *The wicked Mr. Hyde is back. . . .*

Will saw the anger in her face and went on the defensive. "Jessss . . . ," he appealed. "Let's just eat what we get and try to have a good time. Is that too much to ask?"

"Too much to ask?" Jessica barked. She had crumpled her napkin into a little ball in her lap. "First you tell me what colleges I'm supposed to go to, then you plan my SATs for me—which, by the way, I've already taken and kicked butt on—and now you order my meal for me like I'm totally helpless? It's embarrassing, Will!"

"Hey, hey," Will coaxed, reaching for her hands. "I was just trying to help you out and make things run a little smoother."

"What are you talking about?" Jessica asked, her voice rising. Rationality was out the window. "Do you think things will get out of hand if you let me order my own meal? That's the stupidest thing I've ever heard!"

"God! Chill out, Melissa!"

Jessica felt like she'd been slapped. She pulled the napkin off her lap and threw it down on the table. "Take me home," she demanded, steely eyed.

"No, don't," Will said, panicked. "I'm so sorry, Jess. It was an accident."

*Accident, my butt.* Jessica's face was almost purple. "Tell the waitress to cancel the order," she said. "I'll meet you out at the car."


Will flung open his bedroom door, fists clenched at his sides. He saw the football in the middle of the floor and didn't even hesitate. He kicked it as hard as he could in the general direction of the closet. There was a loud crash, and some shirts fell to the floor. But the football popped right back out onto the carpet and lay there, spinning and taunting him. He kicked it again, this time against his desk. The phone fell off and skipped across the floor.

*Settle down before you break something,* Will told himself. He stood there a second, trying to slow his maniacal breathing. The faint sound of the phone's dial tone seemed to be mocking him. He picked it up and rested it back on the desk, his hands trembling.

*You're such an idiot. Such a blithering, drooling idiot. IQ somewhere in the low fifties. Flat-out dumb.*

Will paced across the room. Jessica had made it perfectly clear. *She has a mind of her own, and she doesn't like to be told what to do. She's not Melissa.* So what did he do? He ordered her food without asking, told her where to go to college, and then called her Melissa. Check, please.

Will leaned up against the closet, his chest still heaving. He looked down. There, on the floor, was the still unpacked box of memories that Melissa had dropped off. He could see the old lucky-number-nine jersey leaking out the top of the box. Will felt his taut neck muscles loosen a little. He stooped down and pulled the jersey out of the box. Melissa used to wear it to school on game days—just the jersey and a pair of jeans. It was a little cheesy, now that he thought back on it. But at least he always knew she was really committed to him.

Will backpedaled to his bed, still holding the jersey in his hands. Maybe this was a sign. Not destiny or the hands of fate or anything melodramatic like that. But more than a coincidence at least. Maybe he just wasn't cut out for an independent woman like Jessica. He might need a more old-fashioned, stand-by-your-man type. And Melissa was definitely that type.

*Who am I kidding?* Will thought, tossing the jersey aside. He thought back on how impossible it was with Melissa toward the end of their relationship. It was like jail. He remembered, specifically, sitting right here on this bed after she had attempted suicide. He couldn't go through that again. It was too much pain. Too much guilt. Too much everything.

Will stood up. Tonight was his fault. Jessica had every right to be bitter and walk out on him. And with a beautiful, strong-headed girl like her, she could easily decide to walk out on him for good.

Will grabbed the keys off his bureau. It was time to swallow a heaping dose of pride. He had to prove to himself that he could handle a woman as strong and complex as Jessica. He had to find her and apologize right now . . . before she kicked him to the curb.

# Elizabeth Wakefield

<u>Creative</u> <u>Writing</u>
A Fable Expressing the Theme:
The Transformative Power of Love

Thelonious Weed was the only weed in the Grand Garden. He was not an entirely unattractive weed, with four green stems branching into crystal-laden leaves. But he could not see his own beauty, and he grew up resenting the red roses and happy-go-lucky rhododendrons and ripe tomato plants that inhabited the grounds around him. At an early age he decided to destroy them all, to slowly suck the nutrients from the soil beneath every living plant in his sight.

Thelonious struck the roses first. He moseyed over nonchalantly and set up camp at the majestic plants' base. Day after day he sucked hard at all the nutrients and water at the base of each plant until one by one, the roses wilted and died. When the last rose had sunk down and laid its weak petals against the dirt, she looked up at Thelonious and pleaded for her life. "Why do you insist on killing us?" the rose asked, gasping for breath. "If you lent me just a little morsel of nitrogen, I could survive, and I would be your faithful flower forever." Thelonious, who had grown quite tall from his greedy excesses, just looked down at the rose and laughed. He took one last suck of goodies from the ground and watched the rose sink into the earth.

Thelonious continued his ruthless campaign day after day, plant after plant, until the Grand Garden no longer existed. All that remained was a huge, bitter weed, looking down on his plot of land with hateful pride.

Days went by, and Thelonious grew bored and lonely. All the plants he had killed provided plenty of nutrients for him to prosper by, but it wasn't enough. Thelonious had nothing more to live for—no plants to kill, no one to talk to. He grew increasingly depressed until he no longer wanted to live and simply stopped eating and drinking altogether. What was the point? In no time Thelonious wilted down to the size he had been as a very little boy. His frail, dried-out leaves were scraping the ground now, and his days were numbered.

Thelonious woke up one day from a deep sleep, surprised to find himself still alive. He rolled his weary leaf head over and noticed a small green growth to his right. It was another weed, a young, spry female with oil-soaked leaves and a huge smile on her face. "You don't look so good, mister," Wanda Weed said, batting her eyelashes. "I'll bet you could use a friend." She crept over to Thelonious, snuggled against him, and purred with delight.

A warm, tingling sensation shot through Thelonious—it was like nothing he had ever felt. For reasons he couldn't understand,

Thelonious used his last inkling of energy to reach deep into his roots and pull some nutrients from the ground. At that moment Thelonious decided to live.

And live he did. In the following days Wanda convinced Thelonious to invite surrounding plants and flowers, who had long feared his tyrannical presence, to send seeds to their plot of land. There was plenty of dirt and water and nutrients for all, she explained . . . and Thelonious agreed.

In no time the Grand Garden had returned to its original glory. The roses returned. So did the rhododendrons and the tomatoes, as well as new plants like squash and pumpkins. And to this day, if you look in the Grand Garden, you will see, standing proudly front and center, with Wanda at his side and a big smile on his leafy face—the king of the Grand Garden, Thelonious Weed.

The end

# CHAPTER

## Lingering Tensions

Stanford application. Check. *Oracle* biography column. Check. Job applications. Check. Creative-writing assignment. Check.

Elizabeth put her pen down on the coffee table, satisfied with herself. Only one thing left on the to-do list. She glanced back at the last item. "Convince parents you're worthy of going to the party with Conner." That last one could be a little tougher.

Elizabeth brought two fingers to her lips. She needed a plan of attack. First strategic issue—should she target her mom or her dad? Her dad had enthusiastically helped her with college applications all afternoon, so he was a good candidate. But he was probably up in the den reading or watching golf, so he wouldn't want to be disturbed. Or maybe he would be so absorbed in the relaxing nontask at hand that he would be easy to win over.

Elizabeth heard footsteps in the kitchen. Mom. The sound of pots and pans rustling. The sink turned on, then off. Refrigerator door open, and . . . there! Humming. If she was humming, that meant good mood. Elizabeth walked over to the kitchen door, took a deep breath, and rubbed her hands together.

"Whatcha doing, Mom?" she blurted out nervously. Mrs. Wakefield was sitting at the kitchen table, eating a tuna-salad sandwich. Elizabeth leaned up against the chair opposite her and tried not to fidget.

Mrs. Wakefield put a finger up in the air while she finished chewing. "I was just grabbing a snack," she mumbled. "Want some tuna?"

"No, thanks," Elizabeth said. She searched her mind for some natural segue into the party conversation. Blank.

"It looked like you got a lot done today, Liz," Mrs. Wakefield said. "What all were you working on?"

"Well, Dad helped me with my Stanford application," Elizabeth replied nonchalantly. "And then I wrote a column for the *Oracle,* filled out five job applications, and finished my homework for Monday and Tuesday." Elizabeth checked her mom for a reaction, but she was fixated on her sandwich. "It was a pretty productive day."

"S'great, Liz," Mrs. Wakefield said, still chewing.

"Yeah," Elizabeth responded lamely. Was there no natural way to bring up this party? The silence made Elizabeth feel squirmy, so she pulled out her chair and sat down.

"Mom, I was wondering," Elizabeth started. "Since I've gotten a lot done today and I'm going kind of stir-crazy with homework right now . . ."

Mrs. Wakefield smiled. "Spit it out, Liz."

"There's a party tonight that Conner invited me to," Elizabeth said, "and I'd really like to go."

Mrs. Wakefield put down her sandwich. "Well, you have been working hard and doing all the things we talked about. As long as you're home by a reasonable hour, I don't see why not."

"I can go?" Elizabeth asked.

"Sure," Mrs. Wakefield said. "I'll talk to your dad about it, but I don't think he'll mind."

Elizabeth's face brightened. "Thanks a lot, Mom. Actually, I should probably go call Conner and start getting ready."

"There's just one thing, Liz," Mrs. Wakefield said. Elizabeth froze. "Ask Conner to come in and say hi when he gets here."

"Why?" Elizabeth asked, her heart pounding.

"We like to know the people our kids hang out with," Mrs. Wakefield said. "Your father and I feel like we've been remiss when it comes to Conner, so I'd like to talk to him. It's no big deal, Elizabeth."

*Maybe not to you,* Elizabeth thought. But Conner was going to have a cow. "This is so *Leave It to Beaver,*" Elizabeth complained.

"You're not in much of a position to negotiate, you know," her mother said.

"All right, all right."

Elizabeth walked over and grabbed the portable phone off the wall. She dialed Conner's number while walking into the living room. One ring. Two rings . . . answering machine. *Great.* A machine didn't allow her to use her powers of persuasion. She'd just have to drop the bomb when he pulled up in the driveway . . . and hope he didn't speed off to the party without her.

Jessica blitzed through the front door, her face still crimson with anger. She saw a blur in the kitchen that resembled her mom but rushed straight up the stairs. The last thing she wanted to hear was her mother's rational, consoling voice right now.

"Jessica, are you all right?" Mrs. Wakefield asked from the kitchen.

"I'm fine," Jessica called out in her calmest tone.

She reached the top of the stairs and heard Elizabeth in the bathroom. "Hey, Liz," she said, zooming by.

"Why are you back so early?" Elizabeth asked.

"I just wasn't hungry," Jessica answered, slamming her door. Jessica flung herself on the bed and pounded a pillow. She still couldn't believe he actually said it. *Chill out, Melissa!* As if she hadn't been tortured enough by that girl, Will had the nerve . . . no, that was giving him too much credit. He was just so damn clueless about his own feelings, about the fact that he'd never get over that manipulative *b*-word, that it just slipped out.

Jessica turned over and looked up at the ceiling, her eyes welling up with tears. Why had she expected anything different from such a thumbhead jock like

141

Will? He didn't exactly have a stellar track record. He had lied to her about—or at least failed to mention—having a girlfriend of over three years. He had told his friends that she'd come on to him, then slept with his best friend. Another lie. He had basically taken her on an emotional roller-coaster ride through hell and back, with his psycho ex-girlfriend as the cruise director. Which was why Jessica still had the lingering reputation, in some uninformed circles, of being the slut of Sweet Valley High. And now he was calling *her*, of all people, Melissa. Jessica wiped a tear off her cheek. It just wasn't worth it.

She heard a knock at the door. "Jess?"

"Not now, Liz," Jessica answered tearfully. "I'm not in the mood. Sorry."

There was a long pause but no footsteps. Jessica sniffled, half hoping Elizabeth would try again.

"I just thought I'd mention that I'm going to a Big Mesa party in about ten minutes," Elizabeth said. "It should have a lot of cute male distractions. But I know you're not really into that type of thing."

Jessica raised an eyebrow. Big Mesa party. Boys. That meant Jeremy. *What sweet revenge.* Wait a second. Was she on drugs? Whatever lingering feelings Jeremy had for her were crushed the other day at House of Java. And she couldn't use him like that.

"Thanks," Jessica said. "But I don't think I'm up for it right now."

"All right," Elizabeth said. "I just don't want you

telling me at our twenty-fifth SVH reunion that you should have lived it up a little more your senior year. I don't want that on my conscience."

Jessica rolled her eyes and threw her pillow at the door. She stood up on the bed and checked out her complexion in the mirror. A little streaky, but not irreparable. And it wasn't like Jeremy would completely *ignore* her. He was too nice for that.

Elizabeth sprang through the door. "Come on, Jess—"

They caught each other's eyes and broke into laughter. Jessica bounced off the bed and landed on the edge with her feet on the floor. *Sisters are a good thing,* she thought.

"So, does this mean you're coming?" Elizabeth asked.

"Definitely."

Just because Will forgot her name didn't mean she had to sulk away her Saturday night.

Conner pulled into the Wakefields' driveway and tapped his palm against the horn. After the scene the other night, Elizabeth's front door was taboo territory. He didn't want to suffer any unnecessary flashbacks.

Conner looked out the dashboard window and saw Elizabeth jogging toward the car. She was wearing a short, baby-blue dress that rippled perfectly with her stride. Conner felt a surge of positive adrenaline at the sight of her. He hit the power-lock button to unlock her door.

Elizabeth stopped at Conner's window and gave a little tap. He rolled it down.

"Hi," Elizabeth said. She leaned in and gave him a quick peck on the lips.

"You ready to go?" Conner asked.

"I really have to apologize in advance, Conner," Elizabeth said.

*Uh-oh.*

"I know this sounds ridiculous," she said. "But my parents want you to come in and . . . say hi."

Conner looked her in the eyes, deadpan. Why would she do this to him?

"Please, Conner," she begged. "I'm on such thin ice with them right now. . . . There wasn't anything I could do about it."

"Right now?" Conner asked, even though he knew the answer.

"Please."

Conner sighed and turned off the engine.

Elizabeth's hand guided Conner into the living room, where Mr. and Mrs. Wakefield sat side by side on an off-white sofa. This was too weird.

"Hi, Conner," Mr. Wakefield said, standing up. He stepped forward, his right hand extended.

"Mr. Wakefield," Conner replied. He grabbed his hand and gave it a firm shake, almost tripping over the coffee table in the process. "Good to see you again."

144

"Hello, Mrs. Wakefield," he said, extending his hand to her. "How are you?"

Mrs. Wakefield shook his hand. "Fine, Conner. Good to see you. Please, sit down."

"Sure," Conner said, sitting on the love seat. Elizabeth took the chair next to him.

"Conner, I don't want this to be uncomfortable at all," Mr. Wakefield said.

*You're a little late for that,* Conner thought, returning Mr. Wakefield's earnest expression.

"First of all, I want to apologize for my abruptness the other evening," Mr. Wakefield said. "You were just in the wrong place at the wrong time."

Conner nodded. In his experience with parents, it was better to say nothing than to say something that could be taken the wrong way.

"So, where is this party you're going to?" Mr. Wakefield asked.

"It's at Rivington Lake," Conner replied, maintaining eye contact.

"And what kind of party is it?" Mr. Wakefield asked.

*The fun kind, hopefully.* "I'm not really sure. I just know a few of my Big Mesa friends are going to be there." That didn't seem consoling enough, so Conner added, "But they said it would be pretty low-key."

"Well," Mr. Wakefield said, "I'm sure there'll be alcohol there, and I assume that after what happened the other night, neither of you are planning to partake of it."

145

"Definitely not," Conner replied, keeping his face as straight as possible. Where did this guy get off?

"That's good." Mr. Wakefield looked particularly satisfied by that comment. "And you two understand that if there are any problems—anything at all—you can give us a call?"

"Yes." Conner and Elizabeth said it in unison.

Mrs. Wakefield scooted forward and spoke up. "Okay, then. You two go out and have a good time."

"Thanks," Conner said, standing up. Elizabeth followed his lead, and for a split second their backs were both turned on Mr. and Mrs. Wakefield. In that moment Elizabeth gave Conner a secret smile and mouthed the words, "Thank you."

It somehow made the entire, awkward situation worth it.

Will rapped his knuckles against the Wakefields' front door. *Come on, come on.* He looked through the thin strip of glass beside the door. The living-room lights were off, and so were the kitchen lights. How was this possible? He had only dropped her off an hour ago.

He went to knock again but heard footsteps on the stairs. *Thank God.* He rehearsed the apology he had planned while driving over, prepared to spit it out the moment she opened the door.

He heard a lock unlatch, then another. The door hissed open.

"Jessica, I'm so—"

"Excuse me?" Mrs. Wakefield said, startled.

The blood drained from Will's face. "I'm sorry, Mrs. Wakefield. May I please speak to Jessica?"

"You just missed her," Mrs. Wakefield said. "She and Elizabeth went to a party."

"Really?" Will said. What was she talking about? He hadn't heard of anything going on tonight. "Do you have any idea where?"

"It was at a friend of Conner McDermott's." She looked at Will with a faint trace of suspicion. "Do you know Conner?"

"Yeah, I know Conner," Will replied.

"Well, I think it's one of his friends from Big Mesa," she said. "They said it was out on Rivington Lake."

Will felt his stomach churn. A Big Mesa party— great. That meant Jeremy Aames would be there. Had Jessica totally given up on him already?

"Thanks a lot, Mrs. Wakefield," Will said. He turned to walk away but caught himself midstride. He couldn't just leave Mrs. Wakefield standing in the doorway like that. "Oh, I'm sorry. Could you just let Jessica know that I stopped by?"

"No problem, Will," Mrs. Wakefield said. "Good luck."

"Thanks," Will said, already at the bottom of the stairs.

*Looks like I'll need it.*

# Jessica Wakefield

I wonder what Jeremy thinks about me (if he thinks about me at all). It can't be good. He probably thinks I'm just a fickle chick who wants as many guys doting on her as she can get. Or maybe he thinks I'm totally insensitive. Or cruel. After the other day at House of Java, he's gotta hate me. I would, if I were him.

All right, so he thinks I'm scum. Which sucks because I was just looking at an old list where I ranked the pros and cons of Jeremy versus Will. And since Will has been living up to all his cons, Jeremy comes out looking like a real pro.

Too bad I feel like such an amateur.

## Mating Rituals

"Let's just walk in," Conner said, glancing at Elizabeth and Jessica. He had already rung the doorbell three times, but the radio was blaring too loud for anyone to hear.

The door swung open suddenly. Conner was almost knocked back by the wave of smoke, music, and chatter.

A guy wearing a huge sombrero jumped into the doorway. It looked like Tommy, but Conner could barely see his face through the shadow. "Well, look who's decided to bless us with his presence."

"Hey," Conner said.

"I should have guessed," Sombrero Guy said. "McDermott rolls in with—not one—but *two* hot blondes. Twins, no less. Still got the magic touch, huh?" He hit Conner on the shoulder playfully. Conner checked Elizabeth's face for some reaction and was immediately annoyed at himself. Why did he care what she thought of his past anyway? It was none of her business.

"Please, come in. Welcome to my party," Tommy

continued, ushering them in with his hand.

"Puett," Conner said, stepping into the foyer. "This is Elizabeth and Jessica Wakefield."

"A pleasure to meet you both," Tommy said, shaking hands and giving them both the full-body scan. Conner reflexively grabbed Elizabeth's hand. Why did guys like Puett think they could undress girls with those beady, probing eyes? Conner looked at Elizabeth and noticed how much brighter she beamed now that he was holding her hand.

"Is Evan here yet?" Conner said, ready to move on.

Tommy pointed to the back corner of the party. "Yeah, I think he set up shop back in the corner with the guys."

"All right," Conner said. "I'll catch you later on?"

Tommy took a step back to clear the path. "I'm sure you will."

Conner pulled Elizabeth forward into the throng of people. "I should have warned you about him," he said once Tommy was out of earshot.

"Actually, I thought he was kind of cute," Jessica responded. Conner looked at her in disbelief. "In a sleazy way, I mean," she added, smiling at Conner.

Conner navigated through a sea of shoulders and backsides, keeping his head on constant swivel. Familiar faces were everywhere, and Conner could see that his arrival with two strange, attractive women was causing a ripple of whispers and points. He had already noticed more than one past love interest, but they all seemed too intimidated to approach. Even Amy Esposito, his bold eighth-grade girlfriend, had averted her eyes when she saw who Conner was holding hands with. He felt like he was escorting two models down a runway.

"Yeah, dawg!"

Conner felt a shoulder in his chest and fell back into the girl behind him, almost knocking her over. He braced himself and apologized.

"What's up, Conner?"

Conner cocked his head back to figure out who was hugging him. A dark-complected kid wearing a buzz cut, goatee, and an enormous grin. "Jeff," he said. "You have to be careful with those greetings, my man."

"Just trying to show the love," Jeff said, smiling. Was he always this enthusiastic, or had he already had a couple too many? "So tell me, McDermott, because we're all dying to know. Which one of these lovely young ladies is your girlfriend?"

*Girlfriend.* Conner felt the blood rush to his face. *Please don't use that word.* "Elizabeth, this is Jeff Kulkarni, and he's absolutely not to be trusted," he quipped, refusing to answer the question. He gestured toward Jessica. "And this is her sister, Jessica."

"Nice to meet you," Jeff said, then looked back at Conner and gave him a pat on the back. "You never cease to amaze me."

"I'm going to say hi to Evan," Conner said, pointing. "You want to come with?"

"I don't think so, man," Jeff said, winking. "I've got work to do."

"All right, take care. Good to see you, man."

Jeff walked off, and Conner looked at Elizabeth and Jessica. "Sorry about all this."

"No problem," Jessica said. "I think I'm going to grab a drink and leave the glamour couple to their social duties."

Conner cringed. *Why does everyone want to label us a couple?* "Watch your back, Jess. These guys seem to have their eyes on you."

"I can take care of myself," Jessica said, rolling her eyes as she walked off. Conner steered Elizabeth toward the loud-talking, Evan-led group in the corner. They had turned the living-room couch into Guy Central. There were about eight of them, all scoping the scene, making comments, and periodically bursting into laughter.

"There you are!" Evan shouted, jumping off the couch. He jogged over and one-arm-hugged Conner.

Conner dropped Elizabeth's hand. He had already been hazed enough about the "couple" thing. These guys would slaughter him with it if he gave them the chance.

"What's up, fellas?" Conner shouted at all the guys on the couch, then looked back at Evan.

"Glad you could make it," Evan said. He looked at Elizabeth and smiled. "Both of you."

"Hi, Evan," Elizabeth said.

"So, how's this little shindig been so far?" Conner asked quickly, cutting Evan off before he said something awkward. He hadn't forgotten Evan's short-lived crush on Elizabeth.

"Oh, standard. You know, hanging with the boys and ripping on the masses," Evan said.

Conner laughed. "That's—"

"So, what's up?" Evan interrupted. He flipped his finger back and forth between Conner and Elizabeth. "Are you two an item now?"

Conner glanced over at the couch crew, who were blatantly sizing Elizabeth up and discussing the finer points of her anatomy. He suddenly felt a little nauseous. "I guess you could say that."

"That's great," Evan said mildly.

They all nodded in awkward agreement. Conner could tell from Elizabeth's half smile that she was squirming.

"Conner," she said, perfectly on cue, "I think I'm gonna grab a drink and check on Jessica. Do you want anything?"

"I'll have whatever you're having," Conner said.

*And make that to go.*

*Not Jeremy. Not Jeremy. Definitely not Jeremy. Not Jeremy. Ooh. Not bad. But still not Jeremy.*

Jessica had taken a full lap around the party and hadn't recognized a soul. Just a bunch of girls who glared at her as if she were an alien invading their planet

153

and a bunch of guys who weren't Jeremy. Bad combo.

Even worse was the guilt that followed her around. For every guy who wasn't Jeremy, Jessica felt equal parts disappointment . . . and relief. *You have a boyfriend,* she kept reminding herself. And Jessica had promised herself—four, five, maybe ten times—that she would stop flip-flopping her affections from Will to Jeremy. Stop playing with their hearts and her own. But still, it would be nice, and perfectly harmless, to at least *see* the guy. Maybe she could just admire him from afar. Then she wouldn't have to deal with the look of utter contempt on his face.

She glanced over at the mob scene waiting to get drinks around the kitchen area. Was it worth the hassle? Yeah, probably. She needed a purpose, something to occupy her hands while she people-watched.

Jessica noticed a guy with a football-player's build shoving his way forward successfully and hustled into position behind him. She rode in his wake past hordes of hungry-eyed cup holders, past a sink filled to the brim with cigarette butts and empty cans and soggy napkins.

Just as the punch bowl came into view, Jessica slammed into Football Guy from behind.

He turned around with his chest puffed, ready for a confrontation. When he saw Jessica, his tight jaw loosened into a boyish smile. "You want a beer?"

Jessica eked out a smile. "Actually, I just wanted some of that nonalcoholic punch over there."

"Coming right up," Football Guy said. He grabbed a cup and reached his hand over a couple of heads. "Yo, Ryan, grab a punch for me," he shouted.

*There are benefits to being a woman,* Jessica thought.

"Here you are," Football Guy said, delivering the cup of punch. He looked at Jessica expectantly.

Jessica tried to smile with an extra hint of gratitude. "Thanks."

"You know," Football Guy said, "you are the most beautiful girl here . . . by far."

Jessica took a sip of her punch, blushing slightly. Comments like that were too obvious to take seriously, but it was impossible to not feel a little flattered. "Thanks."

"I know you think that's just a come-on," he added. "But I'm dead serious."

Jessica looked up from her drink at his round, reddened face. He did look dead serious. But he also looked drunk and not particularly attractive. Jessica took a baby step backward, hoping for an easy escape route. She bumped into the person directly behind her and felt a little splash of beer on the back of her shirt. *Great, I'm cornered by the jolly red giant.*

Football Guy closed the distance between them. "What's your name?"

"Jessica!"

Jessica spun around. Elizabeth had pushed her way into the kitchen. She was cramped between two guys, waving her hand.

155

"I have to talk to you," Elizabeth shouted. "It's an emergency."

Jessica turned back to Football Guy. "Jessica's the name, by the way," she said, shaking his hand. "Thanks for the drink."

"Excuse me . . . excuse me." Jessica waded back through the crowd, occasionally catching glimpses of Elizabeth. She caught an elbow to the ribs and almost spilled her punch. *Parties are just too much fun,* she thought.

"Thanks, Liz," Jessica said, finally reaching her sister's side. "You deserve a Purple Heart for that rescue mission."

"No problem," Elizabeth answered. "I really do have something to tell you, though."

"What's up?"

Elizabeth leaned in slightly, her neck stiff. "When I lean my head to the left, look right behind me, underneath the ceiling fan . . . and be subtle about it."

Elizabeth stepped to the side, and Jessica focused in. A band of people walked by, obscuring her view.

Elizabeth looked back at her quizzically. "You don't see—"

Jessica's heart caught in her throat. She could see his profile a few feet away, bathing in the light from the ceiling fan. Jeremy.

Elizabeth straightened up again, cutting off Jessica's view. "Judging by that look, you saw him."

"Yeah," Jessica said. "What should I do?"

"I'll make it easier on you," Elizabeth said, smiling mischievously. She grabbed Jessica's hand. "Take a deep breath . . . because I'm about to walk away."

Jessica glared at her sister and filled her lungs with air. Then she exhaled in Elizabeth's face.

Elizabeth laughed. "Good luck," she said, and walked off.


"Would you call that dancing?" Andy asked, peering out at a couple grinding on the dance floor.

"I think it's some sort of tribal mating ritual," Tia responded. "Hey! That's Angel's old buddy, what's his name . . . Mike Fitz-something."

"Fitzgerald—yeah, you're right."

Tia sighed. "You know, my imagination has been running wild with Angel off at college. When I see a couple going at it like that, I immediately picture Angel doing the same thing with some gorgeous college girl. Or even worse, two gorgeous college girls."

"Yeah, that's more like it," Andy said.

"I'm not kidding," Tia said, punching Andy on the shoulder. "It drives me nuts when he tells me he's going to huge dance parties like the one he's at tonight. I mean, I know Angel loves me, and he would try to be faithful, but it's got to be so hard."

*We've got to get off this topic . . . now.* Andy grabbed Tia by both shoulders and gave her a friendly little shake. "Listen, Tia, because I'm only going to say it once. This is all in your head. You are the one, the only, the love of Angel's life. And that's all there is to it." Andy could see her brown eyes softening with each word.

"That's sweet of you," Tia said. "But you're his friend, and no offense, but you haven't exactly experienced what it's like to have hundreds of cute, smart females throwing themselves at you."

"Great," Andy said. "Thanks for the confidence booster."

Tia didn't even hear him. She was looking right through Andy, her eyes transfixed on nothing. *You're obsessing.* He tried to imagine what she was seeing in her mind's eye. The first image that came to mind was Angel playing volleyball at the Playboy mansion with bikini models running around him, giggling and jiggling.

Andy turned to the dance floor. Maybe he could use the old comedy routine to take Tia's mind off things. "Check out this meathead doing the muscle-bound jock shuffle. That looks like a very energy-efficient dance."

Tia forced out a chuckle.

"And look over here," Andy added. There was a guy in the middle of the dance floor, flailing around like a complete lunatic. "That's somewhere between the funky chicken and the 'I wanna sex you up' dance."

Tia gave Andy a blank look. She wasn't amused.

"And what's this guy's deal?" Andy said, noticing a suave-looking character dancing toward them, both hands raised. "You're Latina. Is that some kind of samba?"

"That's exactly what it is," Tia said, her eyes focused on him. "And he's adorable."

Andy checked out Samba Guy. He did look like a smooth operator. A tall, bald black guy wearing a million-dollar smile and a nicely pressed white linen shirt. Somewhere between Michael Jordan and Tyrese. Good-looking, good dancer—exactly Tia's type.

Andy smelled trouble. If Angel could see the ravenous look on Tia's face, he would lose it. "Tia, I command you to stop salivating at once. It's embarrassing."

"What?" Tia's eyes were still fixed on Samba Guy's gyrating hips. They seemed to be slowly moving toward her.

"I'm Trent," he said, still dancing. "What's your name?"

"Tia."

Andy rolled his eyes at the coy look on her face.

"Would you like to dance?" he asked, presenting his hand.

Tia's face lit up. Her feet were already moving. "Most definitely," she said, laying her hand in his.

Andy watched Tia shuffle off. *Why can't I do that?* he asked himself. He scanned the dance floor. There were a lot of happy, dancing bachelorettes out there. And he wasn't exactly a male model or a samba king, but he had some moves. *Why not?*

Andy started dancing in place, swaying his shoulders to the beat. He noticed a cute, hip-looking girl just a few feet away, grooving in a red wraparound skirt. *Yeah.* He shuffled forward, trying to synchronize his feet with his shoulders. In no time Andy was right beside her.

"I'm Andy," he said, sidling up next to her, his hand extended. "What's your name?"

The girl looked at him, her eyes half-mast. She said her name, but Andy couldn't hear it over the music.

"Excuse me?" Andy asked.

The girl smiled a little and motioned with her finger for Andy to come closer. *I'm in like Flynn.* Andy took a quick shuffle step in her direction. He leaned forward and did a little shimmy step.

"What was your name again?" he asked.

The girl brought her lips right up to Andy's ear, sending a little shiver down his spine.

"*Taken,*" she said, and immediately danced away.

# Andy Marsden

I must be turning into a dork. Because now even <u>parties</u> make me want to study.

But from what I've heard, parties in college will make high-school parties look like church services.

The kind of party I'm talking about stretches the limits of the imagination. Not just your regular frat party. More like one of those cool ragers in an off-campus apartment, thrown by some friend of a friend. In one room scantily clad people are dancing their lives away, soaking with sweat and whooping for no apparent reason. The next room is a smoky, dimly lit lounge room, filled with cozy little love seats and couches meant specifically for passionate interludes. Another room is someone's bedroom, where five or six people are just sitting around with drinks in their hands, laughing about . . . college stuff.

And I'm just going from room to room, making new friends and saying hi to old ones. Everyone understands my witty sense of humor, and of course, they think it's hysterically funny. But because I'm in college now, I have acquired a new sense of intrigue that makes me not just a funny buddy type but a compelling, I-wonder-what's-going-on-in-that-guy's-head type.

What am I doing at this high-school party? I should be home studying right now.

# CHAPTER 11
# He Hates Me Not

"Hi, Jeremy," Jessica said, still holding her breath. *He hates me....*

Jeremy turned around. Surprisingly, his face brightened into a smile. A lukewarm smile, but a smile nonetheless. *He hates me not.*

"Wow," Jeremy said. "What are you doing here?"

*He hates me.* "My sister invited me," she replied, shrugging. *And I knew you would be here.*

"Cool," Jeremy said. "You remember Stan, right?" He gestured at the good-looking jock type to his left.

"Of course," Jessica said.

"Hey, Jess. How's it going?" Stan said.

"Fine," Jessica said. Was it her imagination, or was Stan's tone just the tiniest bit cold?

"And this is Ezra," Jeremy added, pointing at a funky-looking guy with a mop of curly black hair. "Ezra, this is my friend Jessica," Jeremy said. "We work together at House of Java."

*Friends and coworkers?* Jessica nodded at Ezra, trying not to look disappointed. "Nice to meet you."

Jeremy stepped forward, apparently to single out

163

Jessica for conversation. "Are you having a good time?"

Jessica tucked her hair behind her ear. "I was just trying to decide that myself," she said. "So far all I've done is walk around and not recognize people. Oh, and some big linebacker type sweet-talked me when I went to get a drink."

"Just one come-on?" Jeremy asked, tilting his head. "I would expect this crowd to absolutely swarm you. We don't have any Jessica Wakefields at Big Mesa."

"Sure, you don't," Jessica said sarcastically. She took a sip of her punch, not taking her eyes off Jeremy. His aura was so warm and real—she just wanted to grab him and squeeze.

"So, how's your life these days, Jess?" Jeremy asked. "We haven't really talked in a while." There was a hint of regret in his voice.

"It's okay," she replied, trying not to sound too enthusiastic about life without Jeremy. "You know, school and cheerleading and HOJ—nothing special. How about you?"

"Pretty much the same for me," he said.

"Really?" she said. "Are you cheerleading these days?"

Jeremy laughed. "You should see me in my miniskirt."

Jessica giggled, but then they lapsed into a drawn-out silence.

"So," Jeremy started again. "This is a pleasant surprise. . . . Seeing you here, I mean."

"Yeah, it's pleasant seeing you too," Jessica said, smiling. "But it's no surprise, really. I thought you'd be here."

Jessica felt something tug her arm, hard. It wrenched her body around, almost a full 180 degrees. *What the . . . ?* She looked up into a pair of searing gray-blue eyes embedded in a bright red face. Will.

"Let's get out of here," he said, tugging on her arm again. "Right now."

"Conner McDermott?" a female voice said. "Didn't you hear? He's taken. He showed up with some blond chick from Sweet Valley."

Elizabeth stopped in her tracks and ducked behind the stairway. She couldn't miss this little gossip session. Especially considering that she—the blond chick—had a significant role in it.

"You mean, like, a serious girlfriend?" the other girl asked. "Or is it another one of his two-week flings?"

"Well, the word is that this one's for real. Jeff Kulkarni was saying that Conner walked in holding her hand and he had that *taken* look in his eyes. You know, that hazy, happy, far-off look that guys get."

Elizabeth bit her fist to keep from cracking up. Conner had a "happy, far-off look"? Why hadn't she noticed it? She peered around the stairway, determined not to blow her cover. But she could only see the backs of two miniskirted girls facing Evan's crew in the corner and apparently giving the dish on each one of them. This Big Mesa gossip network was just too amusing.

"Evan's still single, though, isn't he?"

"Yeah, I think so. He's cute, don't you think?"

Elizabeth decided she'd heard enough. She started back toward Conner's group, deliberately walking right past the gossip girls. Give them something else to talk about. It was a little irritating to be the nameless, faceless blond chick at the party. But at least she was with It Guy. And at least other people were noticing the *"taken"* look in It Guy's eyes.

As Elizabeth approached Guy Central, she noticed that Conner was the focal point of the group. All the guys were sitting on the couch in a half circle around him, laughing. The only one standing was Evan, who was slapping Conner's back playfully.

One of the guys spotted Elizabeth and, miraculously, the group fell silent. Evan and Conner immediately turned around. Conner's eyes didn't look *taken* anymore; they just looked weary. *Don't let them get to you,* Elizabeth thought.

"What happened, Liz?" Evan asked. "I thought you went to get your boyfriend a drink?"

Elizabeth rolled her eyes at Evan as a couple of guys snickered.

Conner grabbed her arm. "Let's circulate," he said. "I'll catch you boys later."

"You all right?" Elizabeth asked once they were out of earshot.

Conner's eyes were on the floor. "I'm fine."

Elizabeth bent her head down a little. *I'm sick of this cute-little-married-couple crap too,* she wanted to say. But she knew Conner well enough to know he didn't want to discuss it. Maybe she could *show* him, though.

"Come here," Elizabeth said, grabbing his hand authoritatively.

She guided him down the back hallway silently.

"Do you have to go to the bathroom?" Conner asked.

Elizabeth stopped in the middle of the corridor, turned around, and smiled at him. She reached down and turned a doorknob. Conner looked at her, confused, as she pulled him into the dark room.

Will felt a hand on his shoulder. He swiveled his head and smiled. Jeremy Aames had taken a step forward, apparently ready to "defend" Jessica. How noble. He'd been waiting for an excuse to deck this guy. And that little wussy hand on his shoulder was a damn good start.

"She said she doesn't want to leave," Jeremy said. He was in Will's face now. "So maybe you should just take off without her."

Will's smile grew into a Cheshire-cat grin. *I'm really going to enjoy this,* he thought.

"You know what," he said sarcastically. "Maybe you could show me where the door is, exactly?" Will slapped his hand against Jeremy's shoulder a couple of times for emphasis. "Because I have a terrible memory."

Will saw the two guys on either side of Jeremy take a step forward. He took a quick glance at both to size them up. Obvious jocks, but nothing special. With the adrenaline Will had flowing, he could one-punch all three of them like bowling pins. *One, two, three.*

"Listen, chief," one of them said. His tone was calm and diplomatic. "You're a little out of your territory here."

"Thanks for the pointer, *chief*," Will said.

Will turned back to Jeremy. Will's eyes were a little too wide, and he bobbed slightly with each breath. "I'm ready when you are," Will said. His entire body was stiff with violent energy; he just needed a reason to explode.

"Come on!" Will shouted, flinching forward.

Suddenly Jeremy's face was eclipsed by Jessica's. "Don't do this, Will," she said softly. She grabbed his forearms and pushed him back a couple of steps. Will noticed for the first time that a crowd had gathered around them in a semicircle, watching expectantly.

"Let's go outside and talk," she urged, looking up at him with doe eyes.

For some reason, the sight of her made him even angrier. *Who the hell do you think you are?* "Not now, Jess," he said quickly, trying to push away her arms. She stumbled a little, then grabbed his arms even tighter.

"Will!" she shouted. "What are you trying to prove?"

Will looked at her, red faced, then scanned the silenced crowd staring at him. It was a no-win situation. He might be able to deal with Jeremy and his sidekicks, but there were a lot of other guys there, ready to jump in if necessary.

"Let's go outside," Jessica insisted again.

Will stared at her, his eyes cold. *I'll never forgive you for this.* "Don't bother, Jess," he said, slowly backpedaling. "You can just stay here with your new buddies . . . 'cause I'm gone."

He flung Jessica's hands away and stomped off.

"Will!" Jessica yelled. She could see his dark figure in the distance, speed walking toward the Blazer. She broke into a sprint. "Will, wait!"

When she caught up to him, he had the door open and was climbing into the driver's seat. "Will, hold on a second," she said. "Are you okay?"

"I'm fine." Will turned toward her, his eyes fixed on the driveway. "I just came out here to apologize, and when I saw you with him—"

Jessica's breath caught in her throat. She couldn't really blame him for losing it. He had followed her all the way out to a random party, only to find her flirting with Jeremy. She would be angry too.

"You don't have to apologize, Will," Jessica said, taking a step toward him. "But you have to understand, Jeremy was the only person I knew at the party. I was just talking—"

"I really should go," Will interrupted. He still couldn't look Jessica in the eyes. "I need to go home and cool off."

*Why did I have to mention Jeremy's name?* Jessica thought, suddenly overcome by guilt. Will didn't deserve this kind of treatment. Sure, he had made a mistake, and he was a little possessive for her tastes, but at least he came after her.

Jessica grabbed Will's hand. His soft, blue-gray eyes looked so sad, like he had lost something. Jessica couldn't quite understand, but she felt partially responsible.

"You're such a boy," Jessica said, smiling weakly. She put a hand on Will's cheek and pulled him closer. He didn't resist. She kissed him lightly on the lips and waited for the passion to kick in. But his lips felt numb, and his arms were like deadweight on her shoulders. Jessica pulled away and gave him a hug.

"I'm sorry, Jess," Will said, sliding away from her and into his car. "I just need to get out of here."

"Okay," Jessica said, backing away a couple of steps.

"I'll talk to you Monday," Will said.

He slammed the door, leaving Jessica alone in the eerie silence. She felt empty, as if the dark void of the night were somehow inside her as well. Jessica started back to the party and tried to think of something more inspiring. *Monday.* She could patch this whole mess up first thing Monday morning.

As for tonight, she had a more concrete goal—to stay out of trouble. Which, unfortunately, meant avoiding Jeremy Aames like the plague.

# Jessica Wakefield

I shouldn't have been so hard on Will for calling me Melissa. He went out with the girl for three years, for God's sake. Which means he has probably uttered that word, <u>Melissa</u> (it still makes me cringe to hear it), around one <u>million</u> times. It's a natural mistake. Right?

"Liz, why are we—"

Before he could finish the question, Conner felt a wet, tingling sensation on the side of his neck. It shot down his spine and seemed to flower out through his entire body from there—total relaxation. He rolled back his head, basking in the pleasure, and grabbed onto Elizabeth's shoulders for balance.

Her lips worked their way around to his Adam's apple and crept slowly upward, leaving a perfect trail of moisture. They stopped at his chin and hovered there a moment. Conner tilted forward, eyes closed and lips parted slightly.

He couldn't take it any longer. Conner cupped the palm of his hand behind her neck and pushed his lips deep into hers. Elizabeth pushed back, and he could *feel*, deep in his stomach, that she meant it. It was as if she had been storing this kiss up for days, like water constantly on the verge of breaking through a dam. This was the flash flood.

When she pulled away gently, Conner stood there with his eyes closed, reveling in the feeling.

"What brought that on?" he asked, his mind still reeling.

Elizabeth let out a little giggle. "I was sick of feeling like a married couple at a cocktail party."

Conner smiled. *Damn, this girl is pretty cool.* He reached forward blindly, found her hand, and gave it a firm squeeze. He tried to think of something romantic to say, something that might convey the intense, loving ache in his stomach. But thinking about it just made him want another kiss.

"You think we can do that again?" Conner asked, stepping forward and grabbing her other hand.

"You mean, as good as that last one?" Elizabeth asked, backing away coyly.

Conner didn't answer. He just walked with her, hand in hand, toward the far side of the room. There was a sudden crash.

"What was that?" he asked.

Elizabeth started laughing. "I knocked something over."

Elizabeth's laugh was interrupted by a high-pitched creaking sound and a blinding shock of light. Conner turned around.

"Oh, I'm sorry," a dark shadow in the doorway said. "We didn't know you were in here."

"It's okay," Conner said. "We were just leaving."

Conner pulled Elizabeth out of the corner of the room. "Are you all right?" he whispered. She nodded and followed him toward the door.

"It's all yours," Conner said, straightening his hair as he stepped into the light.

"Thanks, man," a tall African American guy said. Conner didn't recognize him. But as the guy ducked past into the room, something struck Conner as odd. He turned around quickly and noticed, from behind, the yellow flowered dress on the girl who slipped in with him. Conner was with her when she bought it.

It was Tia.

This was ridiculous. Where was Elizabeth? Jessica had looked everywhere for her, and the whole party was like a minefield. She had checked the kitchen and narrowly escaped the jolly red giant, who was still sucking down the keg. Then she walked in on a couple making out in the bathroom. She had even checked the basement . . . and gotten bawled out by the host.

The only place left to look was the back porch. If Conner and Elizabeth weren't there, she'd probably have to call a cab. *I'm going to kill Liz when I get home.*

"Jessica."

Jessica spun around and felt her stomach catch in her throat. She was sure he'd left hours ago.

"Oh, hey, Jeremy," she said, backing up a step. *Run, Jessica.* "You're still here?" *Run.*

"Yeah," Jeremy said. He lightly punched the palm of his hand a couple of times. One of Jeremy's nervous gestures. "Listen, I'm really sorry about—"

"No, I'm sorry. Will just gets . . ." Jessica found herself

swimming in the kindness of Jeremy's eyes for a moment, lost. "He just gets a little out of control sometimes."

"I understand," Jeremy said. He looked at her and opened his mouth, then shut it and looked away.

Jessica inspected her fingernails. *What am I doing here? If Will hears about this, it will be* over. "I really should find my sister and get going." She took a step toward the porch. "It was great seeing you tonight, but—"

"I miss being able to talk to you."

Jeremy said it with such conviction that Jessica didn't dare keep walking. Jeremy ran his hands through his hair. "I mean, I don't want to come between you and . . . you know, but it's driving me nuts not being able to at least talk."

"I know," Jessica answered.

Jeremy fidgeted with his fingers a moment, then looked toward the dance floor. A dozen or so couples were swaying to slow R & B music. Jeremy smiled and turned back to Jessica. "Dance with me?" he asked.

Jessica instinctively shook her head. "I can't."

"Come on," Jeremy said. "You know I don't ever dance. This is a once-in-a-lifetime offer." He looked at the dance floor, then back again. "We don't even have to go over there, where everyone will see us." He pointed to the ground at his feet. "We can dance right here. What do you say? One dance."

Jessica looked at the ceiling, faintly smiling.

"Come on."

Jessica sighed and extended her hand. She saw Jeremy's face brighten suddenly, like a sunrise, and couldn't help smiling back. *I shouldn't be doing this.* Jeremy moved forward and rested his hand on the small of her back. Jessica wrapped her arms around his shoulders and started swaying.

Within seconds Jessica felt the night's built-up tension evaporate into nothing. Jeremy's hand caressed her back slightly, like a little massage. The music coursed through her like a hypnotic trance. The faint whiff of Jeremy's cologne soothed her nostrils like aromatherapy. How could Jessica feel guilty about this? It was too innocent, too perfect.

Jessica rested her head on Jeremy's shoulder and noticed a couple of people watching them intently. This would probably get back to Will, but for some reason, Jessica couldn't bring herself to care.

Will stared through his front windshield, seeing nothing. His molten anger had cooled and had been replaced by rock-hard resolve.

There was no denying the facts. He *was* a little pushy with Jessica at dinner. And he *had* overreacted when he saw her flirting with Jeremy. If she hadn't stepped in the way, he would have knocked Jeremy's stupid self-righteous teeth out. Then he would have clocked both of his friends and anyone else who stepped up to the plate. He wouldn't have felt bad about it either. He probably would have insisted that Jessica leave with him.

Those were the facts. Undisputable. He wasn't going to be played for a fool. He wasn't going to apologize to waitresses for being a little snappy. He wasn't going to keep his opinions to himself. That was that.

Will opened his door, stepped onto the curb, and closed it. There was no turning back. He walked slowly, as if pushed by a constant, invisible force. Across the lawn and up the stairs. He stopped at the front door, exhaled, and knocked. There was a long pause, just as he had expected.

Finally he heard a patter of steps on the staircase and the click of a lock. The door creaked open.

"Will," Melissa said with a small, almost satisfied smile. "I was hoping you would stop by."

# WILL SIMMONS

## 11:45 P.M.

Comfort.

That's the difference between Jessica and Melissa.

So Melissa's not the most stable girl in the world. When I'm in her arms like I was tonight, all my worries dissolve into nothing. And now that I've got that back, I don't want to let it go.

# JESSICA WAKEFIELD
## 11:46 P.M.

I've found the perfect guy. His name is Willemy.

He's got Will's romance, the blue-gray eyes, and his raw, sexy masculinity.

He's got Jeremy's caring, sensitive nonpossessiveness.

Unfortunately the genetic phenomenon of Willemy doesn't exist. And until he does, I'm officially stuck in no-woman's land.

# TIA RAMIREZ
## 12:01 A.M.

ANGEL IS GOING TO KILL ME.

# ANDY MARSDEN

## 12:05 AM

*Has anyone seen Tia?*

BFYR 232